THE LUCIFER STONE

'What really matters is the story,' says Flora, when she begins writing about how she and her brother William became involved in the mystery of the Lucifer Stone. And the story she has to tell is incredibly exciting and gripping . . .

It all began one evening when a strange ear-ringed sailor arrived at the London home of Samuel Rolandson, the great magician of the Victorian music halls, to deliver a mysterious warning. But Rolandson had vanished without a trace . . . and when Flora and William, his young wards, set off to warn their guardian, they were swept into a hair-raising adventure to recover a stolen diamond.

'The evocations of Victorian London and Cornwall are both beautiful and convincing but they are not allowed to get in the way of the exciting story which people of nine to twelve should enjoy.'

Times Educational Supplement

HARRIET GRAHAM

The Lucifer Stone

COLLINS · LIONS

First published 1973 by Abelard-Schuman Ltd.
First published in Lions 1976
by William Collins Sons and Co Ltd
14 St James's Place, London sw1

© Harriet Graham 1973

Printed in Great Britain
by William Collins Sons and Co Ltd, Glasgow

FOR MY HUSBAND
JOHN

Contents

1. The Letter

It must have been about half-past seven on that spring evening in 1890 when a tall figure stepped ashore from a fishing vessel in the Port of London. Being a stranger to the city he stopped on the quayside to ask his way and then set off at a steady pace towards Kennington in South London. The business which had brought him was urgent and had to be completed before he set sail again on the morning tide, so he walked steadily, without stopping for rest or refreshment, and he seemed to be unaware of the grey streets through which he passed, or the ragged, white-faced children who played on the steps of the houses.

His own face was browned by sun and sea winds and in his ears he wore gold rings, which made several of the children stop their games and stare after him in curiosity as he went along. Not that he noticed that. His attention was fixed only on the road ahead. Except that every once in a while his hand would reach up to the inner pocket of his coat to feel the bulkiness of the letter which lay there, as though to reassure himself that it was still safe and sound. Once he stopped to ask a crossing sweeper whether he was on the right road for Kennington, and when he had walked on the sweeper stared after him, leaning on his long broom and shaking his head and smiling over the stranger's gold ear rings and the slow, drawling voice with which he had spoken.

Dusk had given way to darkness. The street lamps were all alight, shining like golden heads along the road and, as the man walked on, the foggy air which was creeping up from the river swirled along the pavements and round corners, muffling the sound of footfalls around him and the din of wheels and hooves on the road.

Faces loomed up suddenly. Women, their shawls clutched round them as they hurried home from the corner shop with a jug of milk or a bag of sugar; a boy, pushing a pram filled with kindling and small coal and dragging his sister by the hand; men, spruced and clean, swaggering a little, because it was Saturday night tonight, the best time of the week, and they were going to the Music Hall, or to meet their sweethearts.

As he approached Kennington the neighbourhood grew more cheerful and well-to-do. There were lighted shop windows with elegant, hand-painted signs above them and the terraces of houses that he passed were set back from the road behind spiked iron railings and looked trim and neat. There seemed to be a great many people about too, strolling along the pavements and laughing and talking, so that the stranger felt suddenly shabby and out of place beside so much Saturday evening finery. After asking for directions once more, he turned at last into a quiet street of small terraced houses.

I suppose that's how it must have been, though of course I can't be absolutely sure, not having been there myself. As a matter of fact Flora and I were in the middle of a quarrel at the time, and when the door bell rang I was sitting on top of her on the half landing, holding on to her wrists. The quarrel had started because I'd caught Flora going into my room and filching my counterpane to use as a cloak. She was dressing

8

up as some queen I suppose. Of course I had objected and one thing led to another.

'Promise to put the counterpane back and never take it again and I'll let you go,' I suggested. I thought it was quite magnanimous of me, but Flora shook her head. In spite of being a girl, and only nine, which is two years younger than me, Flora hates to be beaten in a fight and she is quite tigerish when she is roused. I could see by the light which came from the gas lamp in the hall below that she was scarlet with fury.

'Surrender . . . Never!' she hissed dramatically.

It was then that the door bell rang.

Perhaps it was the suddenness of the noise, or the gloom of the upstairs landing. Perhaps it was just that it was evening and dark outside, but as the jangling of the bell echoed through the house and died slowly away I felt a tiny shiver of fear go down my back. It was unusual for anyone to call in the evening. That is because Samuel Rolandson, who is our Guardian, is a professional Magician and so he is out at the theatre where he works every evening, except of course on Sundays. That evening was a Saturday.

I let go of Flora's wrists, got off her stomach and crawled over to the edge of the landing. She wriggled up beside me and together we peered through the banisters. After a moment we heard Nellie begin her climb from the basement, her grumbles growing louder as she approached the hall. The familiar sound of Nellie's grumbly voice made everything seem quite ordinary again and I let out my breath and grinned at Flora in the half dark, but Flora only laid her finger on her lips to tell me not to make a noise.

'A fine time o'night to go ringin' door bells,' Nellie muttered indignantly as she went towards the door. 'Most decent folks are just about thinkin' o' goin' ter bed . . . And so should you be . . . 'oever yer are.' She sniffed.

By the hat stand she paused for a moment and, twitching the maid's cap off the peg where it hung, she clapped it unceremoniously on her head. Nellie only wore the cap when she opened the front door because she had an idea that it was the right and proper thing to do, for neither Flora nor I thought of Nellie as being a servant, and I don't believe that Samuel did either, even though he paid her every month. I suppose that the cap was like a kind of armour for Nellie. She certainly looked as though she was ready to do battle as she swung back the red plush curtain that hung in front of the door, for she gave it such a vigorous tug that all the curtain rings clattered and every red bobble down the length of the curtain shook and trembled.

'And what might you be wantin' . . . and 'oo are yer anyway?' she asked, opening the door a little and peering suspiciously out into the foggy night. Whoever was standing there was tall, for Nellie was looking up, and although neither Flora nor I could see anything because of the fall of the curtain, I heard the low murmur of a voice which sounded like a man's. We guessed by Nellie's answer that he was asking for Samuel.

''E's not in,' she snapped. ''E's out – workin' – at the the-atre, and 'e won't be back till all hours. So yer'll just 'ave ter call again tomorrow.'

Nellie sounded so fierce that I felt quite sorry for the caller, and I suppose he was trying to decide what to do because there was quite a long silence whilst Nellie just stood and stared at him and rubbed at the rheumatism in her back. I remember that I could hear the distant, muffled clip clop of a hansom cab passing at the end of the road, and further away the cry of a man selling oysters. Closer at hand, beside my right ear in fact, Flora was breathing heavily.

'Who is it?' she whispered. 'Can you see?' I shook my head silently. The air from the street was making the gas lamp flutter in the hall below us, so that it cast weird shadows against the wallpaper on the staircase. Then Nellie took something from the caller, and with a curt nod began to close the door. I thought that she looked relieved as she turned round and drew the red curtain back again, shutting out the street and the fog and the stranger.

Flora reached the hall before I did, taking the last six stairs at a bound.

'Who was it?' she demanded, landing at Nellie's feet. 'We couldn't see, could we William?'

'No,' I said, following her down the stairs more sedately. 'The curtain was in the way. Who was it Nellie?'

Nellie ignored me altogether and looked down at Flora. There was a glint in her eye which meant trouble. 'Up yer get, Miss,' she began. 'On yer feet. I suppose yer thought I didn't know yer was up there, the pair of yer? Well I know'd all the time – I wasn't born yesterday, whatever you may think to the contrary.'

She reached out a hand as she was talking and jerked Flora to her feet with surprising strength. Although Nellie is small and rather old and as frail looking as a London sparrow, so Samuel says, both Flora and I know to our cost that she is still capable of giving either one of us a clout that can send us reeling into next week.

'If I opens the front door,' she went on, swinging Flora round and sweeping the dust off the back of her skirt with her other hand, 'then *I* opens the front door, and it's none o' your business to go peerin' through banisters to see 'oo's there, 'cos if it's anythin' wot concerns you – then you'll know soon enough.'

She paused and sniffed and then caught sight of Flora's legs. 'And get those wrinkles out o' yer stockings,' she went on. 'Yer look like something that's come from the workhouse.'

In former days, before she came to look after us, Nellie had been a theatrical dresser, and her years in the theatre had left their mark. Nothing was more likely to infuriate her than a rumpled and untidy appearance, as Flora, who was Nellie's pride and joy, knew pretty well.

'Other kids don't go peerin' through banisters,' Nellie went on, jabbing a hairpin back into her bun. 'Other kids know 'ow to mind their own business.'

'But we aren't like other kids,' Flora said, in a muffled, upside-down voice as she struggled to untwist her black stockings.

'And why aren't yer like other kids, I'd like ter know?' Nellie snapped.

'Well for one thing,' I interrupted, coming to the bottom of the stairs and sitting down, 'we've got no mother, which most children have. And to go on with, Flora and I aren't proper brother and sister – and then Samuel isn't our father, but our Guardian . . .' I was ticking the items off on my fingers in the way that Samuel always does when making out an argument for something and quite enjoying myself until I was stopped short by Nellie letting out a thin, piercing wail.

'Ooh!' she cried, 'Ooh, don't say that! Don't ever say that William!' And her face began to pucker up so that she looked like a sad, old monkey. 'I've done my best, I'm sure I've done my best, but it's not the same – I know it's not the same . . .' And she shook her head from side to side so that several hairpins fell out of her bun, and then she buried her face in her hands.

Some grown-ups never cry at all, but Nellie quite often bursts into tears. Weddings and infant funerals always make her cry and even a sentimental song is enough to make her search for her handkerchief.

Flora looked at me reproachfully. 'How could you, William?' she said. 'You know the thought of us having no mother always makes her cry,' and she put her arms round Nellie and hugged her. 'Don't,' she begged. 'It'll give you a headache, you know it will.'

'But I can't 'elp it,' Nellie wailed. 'Just thinking of yer both, yer poor little motherless babes . . . ooh!'

'But we're not motherless,' said Flora, between Nellie's wails. 'We've got you.'

'I do me best . . . but it's not the same,' Nellie moaned.

'Yes, it is,' I said, picking up the hairpins and going and hugging Nellie as well to make amends. 'It's just the same.'

'Of course it is,' Flora said quickly. 'And we don't want anyone else, ever. Do we William?'

'Rather not,' I said.

In a little while Nellie allowed herself to be consoled and after blowing her nose and wiping her eyes she jabbed the hairpins back into her bun and beamed at us both. 'Well I loves yer anyway,' she sniffed. 'Even though yer are more nosey than other kids.'

'Oh yes,' I said. 'Who was at the door anyway?'

'See what I mean?' said Nellie.

'Do tell us though,' Flora pleaded. 'It's such an odd time for anyone to come.'

'Odd indeed,' Nellie nodded, folding her hands in

front of her. 'And an odd-looking customer 'e was too.'

'Why? What did he look like?' Flora asked.

'Reg'lar pirate,' said Nellie. 'Do you know 'e 'ad gold rings in 'is ears.'

'Truly?' Flora's eyes widened.

'In both ears, mind you. I didn't fancy the look of 'im to tell yer the truth. Never mind. All those years as a dresser stands yer in good stead.' She gave a nod of satisfaction. 'I soon sent 'im packin'.'

'What did he want though?' I asked.

'Well, ter see Samuel of course. Yer didn't think 'e'd come ter see you, did yer? 'E left this letter,' she said, pulling an envelope from her apron pocket and putting it on the hall chair beside the afternoon post. 'And now,' she said, turning to Flora, 'if you've no more questions, either of yer, ternight's 'air washin' night, Miss. The copper's on, the fire's nice and bright for dryin' it and I don't want no excuses, so downstairs with yer, and – ' She held up her hand. 'If you're a good girl I'll tell yer about the time I dressed Miss Ellen Terry as Lady Macbeth, 'cos yer likes that story, don't yer?'

'All of it?' Flora asked cautiously. 'All about the bad luck? And how her hair nearly caught fire?'

'That's right,' Nellie answered, firmly steering her towards the stairs. 'And about the bracelet made like snakes as well – and that's a bit wot you've *never* 'eard before . . .'

They disappeared downstairs, and after a while I heard muffled protests from Flora and orders from Nellie to keep her head down if she didn't want soap in her eyes, followed by the sound of splashing water.

I went over to the chair and looked at the letter lying there. The envelope was long and white and must have had several sheets of paper inside it, for when I picked it up it was quite heavy. It was addressed to Samuel in writing that I was sure I had never seen before, rather spiky and black, and when I turned it over in my hand I saw that the back of the letter was stuck down with sealing wax. Altogether it was the most mysterious looking letter I had ever seen and somehow I think I knew that it was important. I put it back slowly. Then I picked it up again. I inspected it against the light, read the address several times, smelt it and wished that Samuel were here instead of being at the Alhambra Music Hall in Brixton. By the time he came home I should be asleep and so I would have to wait until the morning to find out what the letter contained. Even then, I thought, Samuel might not tell me.

In the end I flipped it back on to the chair again and went downstairs wondering what kind of person would wear gold rings in his ears.

2. Samuel Returns

Downstairs in the kitchen I took my Latin grammar from the dresser and sat down at the table.

I don't know whether every home has a heart to it, but our house in Kennington certainly had. Its heart was the kitchen. Not the back kitchen, of course, because that was small and freezingly cold even in the middle of summer and no one could feel at home in a room that was mostly broom cupboard and larder. The rest of the space was taken up with the sink and draining board, and the old iron bucket which Nellie used for everything under the sun, and which, when scraped across the stone tiles made a noise to set one's teeth on edge. But the front kitchen was always warm and cheerful. Just to walk in and see the dresser with all the blue and white china and gleaming copper along the shelves, and to sniff the delicious smell of a stew in the oven, or of clothes airing on the towel-horse in front of the range made you feel at home.

It was a good, big room too, so that there was enough space for all of us to be doing different things without getting in each other's way. There was a long, scrubbed wooden table in the middle of the room, with chairs round it, and beside the range, where Nellie could sit in it to warm her feet, was the sagging old armchair with the faded rose-patterned cover. There was a rag rug too, all bright red and blue, and a gleaming copper coal box with the fire irons propped up behind it on the other side of the range.

Nellie never allowed anyone to touch the fire except

herself and she kept it going day and night. The only time the range ever went out was when the wind swung round to the north-east. Then it was best to keep out of Nellie's way. There would be nothing but bread and jam for breakfast and only cold water to wash in. Grumbling and muttering and pleading, Nellie would kneel in front of the range, surrounded by newspaper and sticks and coal, trying to coax the fire to burn properly. Sometimes she had to use lamp oil, and Flora and I were ordered to stand back while the great sheet of yellow flame roared and leapt up the chimney. But even when the fire had been re-lighted it wouldn't burn properly when the wind was in the north-east. Instead, it crouched miserably behind the bars, as though it was doing its best to hide from the wind which rushed at it in gusts down the chimney.

That Saturday evening there was no wind though, and the fire glowed golden and scarlet and rose pink behind the bars. It had reached that stage at which it would have been perfect for making toast or, better still, toffee. Not that there was any possibility of doing either that evening, for Flora and Nellie and all the towels and hairbrushes occupied every inch of space on the rag rug.

It wasn't very easy to concentrate on the pluperfect of the Latin verb 'amo' either, because although Nellie had finished telling Flora about Ellen Terry as Lady Macbeth, Flora kept squeaking every time the comb hit a tangle, and every time she squeaked it made me look up and lose my place.

I couldn't help thinking how awful it would be to be a girl and to have to put up with all that fuss, but then Flora is so vain that I don't suppose she minds. Most people think her very pretty and I suppose she is in a way, but it's hard to tell when it's someone you know as well as I know Flora. Usually it's her lovely grey eyes and long, dark lashes that people remark on. Her lashes are very long – and she knows it. Nellie goes on about her hair, too, and says it is the colour of ripe hazelnuts. Of course all this makes Flora very conceited about her looks and if she's ever wanted and can't be found, she's sure to be upstairs in her bedroom gazing at herself in the looking glass.

'My aunt 'ad 'air as long as yours is now,' Nellie said, just as I was getting back to 'Amo' again. 'The one wot lived at Saint Paul's – and till the day she died at eighty-four it was as black as a raven's wing. Not a white 'air on 'er 'ead. Fancy that . . .' Flora wriggled and sighed gustily. 'Not dry yet,' said Nellie. 'Not by a long chalk.'

'Tell me about how Samuel found me then,' Flora suggested. 'You know that always makes me sit still.'

'Oh, not again,' I groaned. 'You must know it by heart, and I'm trying to do this Latin.'

'Well, we've got to get this 'air dry some'ow, William,' said Nellie, siding with Flora. 'If you can't learn in 'ere you'd best go upstairs.'

'It's cold up there,' I grumbled.

'Well, put your fingers in your ears then,' said Flora, giving Nellie one of her special, melting smiles and fluttering her long lashes. Of course Nellie spoils Flora horribly and can't seem to see through her like I can.

I didn't see why I should put my fingers in my ears to please Flora, so I pushed the Latin grammar further down the table and listened as Nellie began, once again, to tell the story of how, one week in December, just before Christmas, she had been dressing Miss Vesta Tilley at the Holborn Empire. Also appearing on the programme was a young Magician who was just beginning to make a name for himself on account of his unusual act. His name was Samuel Rolandson.

'It was during the second house,' Nellie went on, 'and Samuel 'ad just opened – with 'is customary flourish – ' she used the comb as a wand and demonstrated, 'this box. Inside it there was *meant* to be a white rabbit. But . . . imagine 'is utter astonishment when 'e discovered, not the rabbit at all . . . but a baby!'

'Me!' Flora interrupted, her eyes shining. 'It was me!' She always interrupted there.

'Yes,' Nellie nodded. 'It was you.'

'Go on,' said Flora.

'Well – after Samuel 'ad 'eld yer up for the audience ter see, and yer'd got yer round of applause – 'cos they was all highly delighted I can tell yer – '

'Yes?'

'Well, then 'e carried yer off into the wings, not quite knowing what else to do with yer, yer might say, because the whole thing 'ad come as a bit of a surprise to 'im.'

'A jolly nasty surprise I should think,' I interrupted, 'finding a squalling red-faced baby instead of a nice white rabbit.'

Nellie frowned at the interruption and Flora gave me what she hoped was a haughty stare and turned her back.

'Go on,' she said, tapping Nellie's knee. 'Don't mind him.'

Nellie turned to Flora and began again. 'Well, when Samuel gets off into the wings, the first person 'e sees is me, standin' there wiv me mouth open. "'Ere," 'e says, shovin' you into me arms. "Take this will yer . . ." And that was 'ow I come to be left 'oldin' ther baby . . .' She broke off with a shriek of laughter; she always laughed when she cracked that joke.

'Did they clap much?' Flora asked, after a moment.

'Ooh, ever such a lot,' Nellie nodded. 'Yer see, they thought it was part of the act, and 'oever 'eard of a Magician producing a real live baby? Why, they thought it was just about the cleverest thing they'd ever seen.'

Flora gave a sigh of satisfaction. 'And that's how Samuel came to keep me,' she said.

'That's it,' said Nellie, patting Flora's cheek. ''Cos yer brought 'im so much luck. Yer see, from then on the engagements came floodin' in and 'e never was so busy. Well, 'e couldn't very well send yer off to the workhouse, could 'e? Besides, there was 'is Nibs 'ere – ' she jerked her head in my direction. ''E was already part of the act, yer might say, gettin' under foot back-stage and bein' spoilt ter death into the bargain. So Samuel thought 'e might as well make a proper job of it and take on the two of yer. That was when 'e asked me if I'd like ter join the party as well. 'E found this 'ouse, and 'ere we all are. Of course in the early days we 'ad to 'ave a lodger on the top floor, otherwise we'd never 'ave made ends meet.'

Flora was staring into the fire. 'Suppose,' she said, her voice sinking to a whisper, 'suppose Samuel had sent me to the workhouse.'

'Suppose he'd sent me there too,' I said.

Flora twisted her head away from Nellie's combing and turned and looked at me. For a moment we stared at one another in silence. We quite enjoyed scaring ourselves when we were sitting snugly round the kitchen fire at home. But we never passed the grim, grey building in Kennington Road without a shudder, for we both knew that if Samuel had been a different person we would have been workhouse children like the ones we glimpsed through the heavy iron gates

20

which shut them away from the outside world. We would have had short haircuts and shapeless clothes like them, and there would have been no kitchen fire to sit round then, or any of the other things we enjoyed. No dancing lessons for Flora, or visits to the theatre to see Samuel backstage and watch him making-up. No rides on the tram to have tea at the Army and Navy Stores, which was our special treat. No Nellie. And no Samuel either.

'I wonder what really made him decide to keep us,' I said.

Nellie shook her head. 'Samuel Rolandson,' she said gravely, 'is a very unusual man. Like the Almighty,' Nellie added, pointing at the ceiling, 'Samuel Rolandson moves in a mysterious way 'is wonders to perform.'

'Wouldn't it be marvellous,' I said, leaning my elbows on the table, 'if we could do something for *him*.'

Flora nodded. 'Something really special.'

'A thing of incstimable service,' I said.

'Yes, yes,' Flora cried excitcdly, kneeling up and putting her hands together. 'Like the knights at the court of King Arthur.' Flora was rather keen on King Arthur just then. Sometimes she played at being Queen Guinevere and sometimes the Fair Elaine, but best of all she liked being Sir Galahad in search of the Holy Grail.

'That 'air's dry now,' Nellie interrupted, bringing us down to earth again with a bump and whisking the towel from Flora's shoulders. 'And if either of yer'd like to do anything for *me* – yer can get a couple of spoons out of the dresser drawer, 'cos it's time for yer supper.'

Flora and I ate without talking. I had opened my Latin book again and was mouthing the pluperfect between spoonfuls of soup. The only sound was the ticking of the clock and the murmur of the coal shifting in the grate, for Nellie had gone suddenly and soundly to sleep in her old armchair. Flora was in a daydream which could have been about King Arthur but was more likely to be about herself dancing in the middle of a huge stage and wearing a coronet of pink rosebuds and a Columbine dress. Flora has ambitions to go on the stage and talks about it being her destiny, which I think is all tosh, and only because of the way she was found by Samuel. Samuel is soft with her, too, just like Nellie. And so, while I was ploughing through my Latin grammar once a week with Mr Willoughby, Flora went to a dancing class and capered round with a whole lot of other girls.

I hated having Latin lessons and I don't think that Mr Willoughby liked it much either, because he spent most of the time looking out of the window, except when I made a mistake. Then he would look at me sadly and give an enormous sigh. It would have been better if he had sometimes lost his temper, but he never did. He lived at the top of a shabby, brown house in Kennington Road, in a room which was always cold, and he wore grey mittens to keep his hands warm. I think that he had fallen on hard times and that was one of the reasons why Samuel paid him to teach me Latin. The other reason was that Samuel hoped. one day, to send me to a good school. If ever Mr Lucifer turned up, he said, I would get a proper education.

Mr Lucifer was our excuse for putting off all things that we couldn't afford but hoped that we should have one day. 'We'll see about that when Mr Lucifer comes home,' Samuel would say when one of us asked for something that was too expensive, and although there

22

was hardly ever a week when Samuel wasn't working, we were still quite poor and there always seemed to be a great many bills. If things got really bad Nellie would trim hats for a bit of extra money.

Flora was still stuck in the middle of her daydream with an aggravating secret smile on her face, and when I kicked her under the table she jumped.

'I wish you could see yourself,' I grinned. 'You look like the cat that got at the cream. I suppose you were thinking how clever you were to be discovered inside that box?'

'Well, at least I wasn't picked up from a dirty old wagon in the middle of Africa, like you,' she retorted.

'Or were you whirling round some stage?' I went on, ignoring her jibe about the wagon. 'Did they clap you much? Did you get an encore?'

That was too much for Flora. She went rather red and grabbed my Latin book. I saw what she was going to do, of course, but I was too late to duck and I was still rubbing my head as she flounced to the door and went out, banging it behind her.

'What's goin' on now?' Nellie asked, opening one eye suddenly and sitting up very straight.

'Flora hit me,' I said.

'Oh, yer poor little soul,' said Nellie sarcastically. 'And you're only about twice her size too.'

'She began it,' I grumbled.

'Just because me eyes is closed it doesn't mean I'm asleep yer know,' Nellie said, giving me a sharp look. 'Now off ter bed wiv yer and no more of yer nonsense. You two will be glad of each other one day, you mark my words.'

Actually I thought quite a lot of Flora, and I only teased her because sometimes she really needed taking down a peg or two. When she wasn't showing off, or being conceited about her looks or her ambitions to go on the stage, Flora was all right. In fact she could be quite sensible when she wanted to and sometimes she was good fun. Halfway upstairs I was sorry that I had ragged her, and I put my head round her bedroom door to say so. Flora still shared a room with Nellie and she was in her nightgown, posing in front of the looking glass as usual.

'My Lady,' I said, going into the room and dropping on one knee in front of her, 'forgive my uncourteous and unchivalrous words, not fitted to your beauty's ears.' It was easier to say sorry that way.

'Arise, Sir Lancelot,' Flora answered. 'Those words shall not be thought on more.'

'Do you realize,' I said, standing up and rubbing my knees, 'that Samuel will be at home all next week because he's having his wisdom teeth taken out?'

'Oh wonderful, beautiful, wonderful!' Flora began to sing, waltzing round the bedroom and waving her hairbrush about.

'If you go on like that,' I said, 'you'll get giddy and fall over.' But I knew how she felt because it was the best treat in the world for us when Samuel had a week off. It meant that he was at home every evening and there was no one in the world better at inventing games than Samuel, and he didn't seem to mind playing them either, unlike most grown-ups.

'Poor Samuel,' Flora said, suddenly stopping. 'Do you suppose the teeth will hurt much?'

'Only to begin with,' I said.

'William –' Flora said, suddenly sitting on the edge of her bed and changing the subject, 'do you ever wonder about your mother? What she was like, I mean?'

'Yes,' I said. 'Sometimes. Don't you?'

Flora nodded and looked at her toes. 'I've been wondering if it was my mother who put me in that box,'
she said. 'And then if it was her, why she did . . .'

After a moment, as Flora was still staring at her toes,
I said rather gruffly : 'Well I tell you what, not knowing, you can imagine what you like, can't you ? What
I wonder mostly is whether my mother was Dutch
or English. Which do you think ?'

'I think,' said Flora, looking a bit more cheerful and
studying me with her head on one side, 'I think Dutch,
because your face is so long and your nose turns up
at the end in that funny way. That's not at all English
you know.' I looked at myself in Flora's glass, but it
didn't help really because I just looked like me as usual.

'Well, I don't suppose it matters much,' I said,
going to the door. 'I'm English now all right. As English
as you.'

The way in which Samuel came to find me was
almost as strange as the way in which he came to find
Flora, but quite different. He was in South Africa at
the time, though what he was doing there he would
never say. He had been away from England for over
ten years, first of all in India where he was in the army,
and then, later, in South Africa. It must have seemed
a long time to be abroad and perhaps he was homesick.
At any rate he had decided to return home.

The journey to the coast was very dangerous, because at that time there was a war going on between
the native Zulus of South Africa and the English and
Dutch settlers who had gone out to live there. Samuel
travelled with a party of people, both English and
Dutch, and they had to go across country, far from
any towns or villages and knowing that they could
be attacked at any time. The women and children
travelled in the covered wagons and the men rode. I

suppose the journey must have taken a long time.

One night, not long before midnight, they were attacked by the Zulus and Samuel says that when morning came the only survivors were himself, and a baby who had remained unnoticed under one of the wagons during the battle. Of course, the baby was me. Samuel made a sling and strapped me to his back, and collecting together all the water he could find, he set off on horseback. He never expected to arrive at the coast, but by some miracle he did, and somehow I had survived as well. He tried to find out who my parents had been, but no one seemed to know and in the end he brought me to England and adopted me legally.

It was then that he went into the Music Hall. Of course to begin with he wasn't The Astonishing Roland-son, which he was later to become, but only a Magician's assistant learning the tricks of the trade. But before long he was able to start his own illusionist act, and it must have been soon after Flora's appearance on the scene that he began styling himself 'The Astonishing Rolandson and his famous Disappearing Doves'. From then on he wore the black, pointed beard and moustache and the top hat and opera cloak, just as it is drawn on the bills which hang outside the theatres.

He did a great many tricks, with rabbits and glasses of water and coloured silk handkerchiefs, but it was the doves that the audiences liked best. First of all he magicked them into existence from under his hands and round the back of his collar and out of his pockets, so that even Flora and I, standing in the wings at the side of the stage and watching, which we were some-times allowed to do, thought that it must be magic. Then, when he had assembled them all on a gilded stand, he would make them disappear again. With the first few, he just held them in his hands again, stroking each one for a moment, and then – the next second – his hands would be empty. The dove had gone. When he reached the last three doves, though, he would put one on each shoulder and the third on the crown of his top hat. There would be a pause; a roll of drums. Then the doves would fly upwards, a little way only, their fluttering shapes snow white against the blackness of the stage, and the next second they had vanished. Samuel would be alone in the middle of the stage.

It was a trick, of course. Flora and I had once plucked up courage to ask Samuel how it was done, but he only shook his head and smiled. As he's always telling us, Magicians have to keep their secrets to themselves.

It was only when I climbed into bed that I remembered the letter again. I thought about it sitting there, on the chair in the front hall, and I thought about the mysterious stranger who wore gold rings in his ears, and the more I thought about it, the odder it seemed. I was sure that there was a perfectly ordinary explanation, which Samuel would tell us in the morning, but trying to think what it might be kept me tossing and turning until my bed was furrowed and ridged and I had to spread my feet to the very edges to find a cool space for them. After a while I heard Nellie come upstairs, and then I heard her bedroom door close. I heard the church clock half a mile away chime eleven.

I was still awake when the hansom cab stopped at last outside our front door, and I scrambled out of bed and went over to the window. Below on the pavement I could see Samuel's familiar figure; the dove basket and the tall black case were beside him on the pavement. I watched while he paid the cabby, and when he turned round and picked up the case and the basket I could see by the light of the street lamp how tired he looked. I suppose that it was because I had been thinking of him in his beard and moustache and top hat that he looked so commonplace and unmagical.

I crept back to bed and turned my pillow to the cool side. I heard Samuel close the front door and I thought of him picking up the letter and opening it. I half wondered whether to go down there and then and ask him what was inside it, but he wouldn't have been pleased to find me still awake, and I remember thinking as I drifted off to sleep that it wasn't long to wait until the morning.

3. The Only Way

In our house the signal that it was time to get up was the sound of Nellie riddling out the kitchen range. The din seemed to travel up through the whole house so that it could be heard in every room and it woke us up pretty thoroughly every morning. Flora and Nellie and I had our breakfast together in the kitchen, and Samuel had his on a tray in his room.

As I did up my shirt buttons and combed by fingers through my hair that Sunday morning, I was thinking of how quickly I could eat my breakfast and feed the doves, which it was my turn to do that day, so that I could go up and see Samuel. I had remembered about the man with the gold rings in his ears and the letter that he had brought as soon as I woke up.

Our routine in the mornings was always the same, even on Sundays. When we had finished our own breakfast, Nellie took Samuel's up to his room on a tray, and we went with her. By then Samuel would be up, strolling about in his dressing-gown, shaving and smelling of soap, with a towel round his neck. The fire would be burning brightly, too, because Nellie lit it before we had our breakfast. Samuel had the same things on his tray every morning: a boiled egg, plenty of toast, butter, and marmalade of the thick, dark sort, and tea. The tray was put on the little card-table in front of the fire, and while Samuel ate, Flora and I would talk to him.

Most grown-ups seem to be always rushing about and only giving you a quarter of their attention if you try to talk to them. But Samuel isn't like that. He really listens properly, and always seems to know if we have any worries; sometimes he even knows what they are before we've told him, which is another kind of magic that he's good at. Then, too, he gives us sensible answers to questions, any kind of questions, even ones that most grown-ups would consider the most fearful cheek. That's why I knew he wouldn't mind me asking him about the letter.

It wasn't until I got inside the kitchen door that I realized something was wrong. Flora was standing in front of the range in her stockinged feet while Nellie, who was looking flushed and flustered, did up the buttons down the back of her dress.

'But where can he have gone?' Flora was saying.

'Where's who gone?' I asked.

'Oh, there you are William,' said Nellie, looking at me and then giving Flora a sharp slap to make her stand still. 'A fine how d'ye do this is. Samuel's gorn off and left us.'

The idea was so absurd that if it hadn't been for the look on Nellie's face I would have burst out laughing. 'But where's he gone?' I asked.

''Ow should I know?' Nellie exclaimed. 'All I know is 'e's not nowhere in the 'ouse, and 'is bed's not been slept in neither.'

'But that's silly,' I said. 'Samuel wouldn't go away without saying something.'

'That's what I think,' Flora nodded, sitting down at the table and reaching for the milk jug. I wouldn't say Flora is exactly greedy, but she does like meals to come at the right time.

'Well whether you think 'e'd go off or not – 'e 'as,' said Nellie, going even redder and jabbing a stray hairpin back into her bun.

30

'Well, I know he came home last night,' I told them.

'How d'you know?' Nellie asked, looking sharply at me.

'Because I was awake. When I heard the hansom drive up the street I went over to the window, and I saw Samuel outside on the pavement.'

'You might have been dreaming,' Flora suggested.

'No, I wasn't,' I frowned. 'But if you don't believe me, go out and look in the yard. If the doves are there we'll know he came back. I'm going upstairs to look in his room.'

Samuel's room was empty all right. It had that tidy, depressing look that rooms have when their owner has left and means to be away for some time. His dressing-gown and slippers had gone. So had his sponge and his shaving brush. His little travelling clock wasn't there either, or the copy of Bacon's *Essays* which he always kept on his bedside table, except when he slipped it into his pocket to read on train journeys. There was no doubt about it. Samuel had gone away.

I stood in the middle of the room and I felt as though the world had turned upside down. I simply couldn't understand why Samuel should go off without saying anything to any of us, because it was so unlike him. And if he'd come back home last night, which I knew he had, then when had he left? The only thing that was really clear was that it all had something to do with the man with the gold rings in his ears and the letter that he had brought.

I turned to go back downstairs to the others, and it was then that I saw it. Propped up on the mantelpiece, where Nellie should have noticed it as soon as she put the coal bucket down beside the fireplace first thing that morning, was a letter addressed to all three of us in Samuel's writing.

'Look!' I shouted, racing back to the kitchen and waving the envelope triumphantly. 'He did leave a note. I knew he wouldn't go off without telling us.'

'Wherever did you find that?' Nellie asked, sitting down plump in the nearest chair.

'On the mantelpiece, of course,' I said. 'I can't think how you missed it.'

'You were right about the doves too,' Flora nodded. 'They are there.'

''Oo's that letter addressed to?' Nellie asked, peering at it.

'All of us,' I said. Flora jumped up and down and tried to get it from me, only I snatched it away. 'My name's first,' I told her.

'Well you'd better open it then,' Nellie nodded, 'and read it out loud.'

Inside the envelope there was a single sheet of paper.

' "My dear William, Nellie and Flora",' I read, ' "I am sure you will be surprised to find that I have gone away, but please don't be alarmed. I have had to leave suddenly on urgent business, and did not even have time to warn you of my departure. I am not yet certain how long I shall be away, so I have sent word to the Holborn Palace of Varieties that I shall not be appearing there the week after next ..." '

''E's never goin' ter be away for two weeks, is 'e?' Nellie interrupted, holding the teapot in mid-air.

'It looks like it,' I said.

'Go on, then,' Flora said.

' "As you know",' I read, ' "this coming week was a free one for me anyway. Will one of you please run round to Mr Bragg, the dentist, on Monday morning and tell him that I shan't be able to keep my appointment after all? The wisdom teeth must wait. You will find all the money you can possibly need in the tobacco jar in my room. In case of real emergency you could send a letter to: Spindrift, Newlyn, Penzance, Cornwall. My lawyers, by the way, are Bartlett, Bartlett & Pearce, 69, Lincoln's Inn Fields. And that, I think, is all you need to know. Take care of each other, and don't worry. I shall be back soon with exciting news for all of you. Affectionately, Samuel." Wait a minute,' I said, before Nellie could interrupt, 'there's a p.s. too. It's for me. It says, "William: I see that you need a new jacket." He must have noticed the holes in the sleeve. "Please go to Finniman and Hardy in Kennington Road and buy yourself one. Nothing too lavish, and ask them to send me the bill. p.p.s. Don't forget to feed the doves." '

'Well!' Nellie gasped, taking the letter from me and fanning her face with it. 'Well, I never did! Did you ever 'ear of such a thing. Creepin' off in the middle of the night like that, wiv never a word to none of us, and goin' for two 'ole weeks. Now 'owever shall we manage all that time I'd like ter know. 'And me my shawl from the chair, William, there's a good boy, I've come over all cold. And Flora, stop chopping that loaf about, that's your third slice and you're cuttin' it slant.'

'It tastes just the same,' said Flora, reaching for the butter. 'What do you suppose Samuel's gone for anyway?'

'Well, 'ow should I know?' said Nellie crossly. 'Goin' off and leavin' us like that. Suppose one of yer was ter be took ill.'

'Haven't you any idea why he could have gone, Nellie? Any idea at all?' I asked.

'No,' Nellie snapped. 'I 'ave not. But if I 'ad 'im 'ere now I'd give 'im a piece of my mind, I can tell yer that.'

Flora stopped licking the jam off her fingers and

stared into the distance. 'I think he's gone off on a quest,' she said dreamily.

'Don't be silly,' I told her. 'This isn't the Court of King Arthur. Whatever Samuel's gone for, it's quite clear it must have something to do with that letter that arrived last night. But what could possibly have been in it to make him go all the way to Cornwall?'

'Cornwall did yer say?' Nellie asked, looking at me.

'Yes. The address in the letter,' I said, pointing it out to her.

'Ah,' said Nellie, suddenly looking much relieved. 'Now I b'lieve 'e's got a sister down there. Paints pictures or something. Mind you, I've never seen 'er, but I know Samuel writes to 'er from time to time.'

'I never knew Samuel had a sister,' I said, looking at Nellie suspiciously, wondering whether she'd made it up.

'Nor did I,' said Flora.

'Children don't know everything, though there's some as'd like to,' Nellie retorted sharply. 'She'll 'ave been taken ill, I shouldn't wonder, and 'e's 'ad ter go down and see 'er.'

'Perhaps,' I said doubtfully. 'But why for two weeks?'

'And what about the exciting news?' Flora put in.

'And why make such a mystery of it?'

Nellie rubbed at the rheumatism in her back and frowned. Then she suddenly stood up and began shovelling coal on to the fire with a great deal of bustle and clatter, so that I knew she was worried.

'Anyway,' I said soothingly, 'we can manage all right. Samuel's been away before and two weeks isn't all that long.'

Flora nodded. 'And we'll be as good as gold, won't we, William? Make our beds...'

'And fetch in the coal.'

'I'll wind the clocks,' said Flora.

'And I'll clean the boots,' I said.

Nellie threw the shovel back into the coal bucket and wiped her hands on her apron. ''Course we'll manage,' she said. 'But what I'd like ter know is – if 'is sister's been took ill why they didn't send a telegram instead of sending a letter by 'and.'

We looked at one another in silence and I remember that the ticking of the clock on the dresser suddenly seemed to be much louder.

Our silence was broken by the sound of someone knocking sharply on the kitchen window. We all looked round and Nellie gave a shriek. 'Lawks a mercy! It's 'im again.'

'Who?' Flora asked, jumping up.

''Im wot brought the letter last night,' said Nellie out of the corner of her mouth and still staring at the face which peered at us through the window from the front area outside. 'Wotever shall we do?'

'We'd better see what he wants,' I said.

'No!' Nellie grabbed my arm. 'Don't you let 'im in 'ere.'

'We can't very well leave him standing out in the area,' Flora said, reasonably enough. 'Besides he's got something to tell us. He's making signals through the window.'

'We could ask him what he wants,' I suggested, 'without letting him come in.'

'Well, don't you open the door more'n a crack, mind,' Nellie muttered, grabbing the poker and hiding it under her apron. 'Don't you let 'im in. Understand?'

Flora opened the door an inch at a time. 'Yes?' she asked, staring up at the tall stranger. 'What do you want?'

After his mysterious arrival the night before and the way that Nellie had taken against him, I think I expected to see a gigantic, black-cloaked figure with a scar from cheekbone to chin and a cutlass tucked into his belt, pirates being the only people I could think of who wore ear rings. But in the cold, bright light of the early morning, standing outside our kitchen door and staring in at us all with a pleasant grin, the stranger didn't look at all like a pirate. It was true that he wore gold rings in his ears, but for the rest he had on a faded blue, canvas smock and a canvas cap to match, and his trouser bottoms were tucked into sea-boots, and I think I guessed almost at once that he was a fisherman. He pulled off his canvas cap and smiled down at Flora, and he had the bluest eyes I had ever seen.

'Well,' said Nellie sharply, pushing Flora to one side before the man could speak. 'What's your business? Yer can't keep pesterin' us like this, yer know.'

'Begging thy pardon, ma'am,' said the stranger, speaking very pleasantly and respectfully as he looked down at Nellie, 'but I've come most urgent to see Mr Samuel Rolandson.' He had a soft, drawling way of speech, not at all like a Londoner, but it seemed to suit the way he looked.

'Well yer can't see 'im, and that's that,' Nellie said, beginning to shut the door. The stranger put out a huge, brown hand and held it against the door.

'Thy pardon again,' he said apologetically, 'but I've important news for Mr Rolandson as'll not wait. So if you'll kindly tell him that Joel Tregarth would like a word with him, early as it is, I'd be obliged to 'ee.'

'Get yer 'and off that door, will yer,' Nellie gasped. 'Yer can't see 'im if 'e's not 'ere, can yer? Now off yer go, or I'll call the police,' and she leant all her weight against the kitchen door in a vain attempt to shut the stranger out. There is no knowing what would have happened next if Nellie had not dropped the poker, but at that very moment it slipped out from under her apron and fell to the floor with a clatter. Without thinking, she bent down to pick it up, letting go of the door as she did so. The stranger, who had been leaning all his weight against it from the other side, sent it flying open and landed, like a huge, sprawling giant on our kitchen floor.

'Oh!' Nellie gasped in horror. 'Now look, will yer! Just see what yer've done now. Whatever next!' The stranger grinned up at Nellie as though he knew quite well how absurd he must look, and Flora started to laugh and then put her hands over her face to hide it.

'Reckon that's not the way to go visitin',' he said good naturedly, clambering to his feet and rubbing his right elbow tenderly. 'Bang on my funny bone, too.'

'Well I'm sorry if you 'urt yerself,' said Nellie, 'but yer'd no right to go leanin' against our door like that . . .'

'Here I am, any road,' the stranger said, giving us all a smile. 'So perhaps I could see Mr Rolandson – if you've no objection.'

'Look,' I said, stepping forward and speaking for the first time, 'we've already told you, only you don't seem to understand. Mr Rolandson isn't here. He's gone away.'

The man stopped smiling. 'Gone!' he exclaimed in dismay. 'Gone already by thunder and codfish! That's bad news indeed,' and he shook his head and whistled softly through his teeth. 'I'm too late then.'

'He's only just gone,' said Flora, looking quite concerned herself. 'He left us a letter saying he'd be away about two weeks. Look, here it is, on the table.'

'I didn't expect he'd have gone so soon though,' the stranger said.

'P'raps yer wouldn't mind tellin' me what all this is about, Mr – er – wot's yer name?' said Nellie.

'Tregarth, ma'am. Joel Tregarth.'

'Well, Mr Tregarth, first of all yer arrive at dead o' night askin' ter see Mr Rolandson, and yer leaves a letter instead. Next thing we know – Mr Rolandson's gone – vanished – ' Nellie waved the poker rather wildly. 'And just as we get used ter the idea of that, 'ere yer are again askin' ter see Mr Rolandson again. What's your business, I'd like ter know? Let's get it over once and for all – ' She took a step towards him and brandished the poker under his nose – ''Cos I'm sick of yer turnin' up like a bad penny.'

For a moment Joel Tregarth didn't answer. His brow was furrowed in thought and he didn't even seem to notice the poker as he shook his head silently from side to side.

'Is it very important then?' Flora asked, giving his sleeve a little tug.

'I reckon it is,' he nodded, looking down at her. 'I reckon it's as important to Mr Rolandson as a storm at sea would be to me. Or a patch of rocks hidden under the water and just waiting to take the bottom off my boat. I've walked all the way back from the Port of London this morning, just to see Mr Rolandson, I thought it was that important. And now he's gone, so it seems that I've missed him as well as the tide, and the question is, what's to be done next?'

I think by now it was clear to all of us, even Nellie, that Joel Tregarth was no villain. What was more, his business with Samuel was obviously urgent. Nellie's face softened a little and she threw the poker back into the coal box. 'Well,' she said, 'since yer've come such a great way you'd best 'ave a cup o' tea. Then perhaps yer can tell us what it's all about. Flora, pour some tea for Mr Tregarth . . . William, pull out a chair so 'e can sit down and take the weight off 'is feet.'

Joel Tregarth thanked Nellie, and when he had lowered himself on to one of our kitchen chairs he drank two cups of tea, wiping his mouth on the back of his hand several times, but he seemed in no hurry to tell us his business.

'Well?' said Nellie at last. 'It's time you explained yerself, yer know.'

'Trouble is, ma'am,' Joel Tregarth said, looking quite perplexed, 'my business with Mr Rolandson is confidential. For his ears only, you might say, and I'm afraid I'd be doing wrong if I was to tell anyone but him.'

'Twaddle!' Nellie replied shortly. 'And if you've been leadin' us up the garden path, there will be trouble and no mistake. Mr Rolandson don't 'ave no secrets from us. We're 'is family.'

'I'm mighty glad to hear it, ma'am,' said Joel Tregarth with a nod, 'and that being the case you'll know the business that's taken him down to Cornwall.'

There was a moment's silence. Nellie opened her mouth and then she closed it again and I could see that Mr Tregarth was watching her pretty closely.

'Look here,' I said, breaking in and leaning across the table towards him, 'if Samuel hasn't told us about this – business – ' I waved my hand, 'well, it's only because he had to leave in such a hurry, and he didn't really have time to explain.'

Flora nodded. 'William's right,' she said seriously, 'and if what you've got to tell him is all that important, then I think we ought to know, ·o that we can decide what to do.'

'After all, if it's important to Samuel, then it's important to us,' I added.

Joel Tregarth sat, looking perplexed and undecided and staring at each one of us in turn, shaking his head but not saying a word, until at last Nellie grew impatient.

'Now look 'ere, Mr Wot's-yer-name, either tell us what's goin' on, right 'ere and now, or else get out o' my kitchen and go after Mr Rolandson yerself wiv your confidential news. Yer know where 'e's gone, 'cos yer said so just now.'

'I would ma'am. Believe me, I would,' Joel Tregarth answered, speaking very solemnly and looking straight at Nellie. 'But as you know I came to London by fishing boat, up the English Channel, and even with a fair wind behind me it'll take me three days to sail back again to Penzance. And that'll be too late.' He leaned forward. 'This news I have for Mr Rolandson only came my way last night, some time after I'd brought him the letter. But believe me, ma'am, if Mr Rolandson's plans are to go aright, and I'm sure we all wish him that, then, by thunder, this packet I have here must reach him tonight. And I'm blessed if I see how it's to be done . . .' And Joel Tregarth ran his fingers through his shaggy hair and looked at us all with an air of consternation, while Flora and Nellie and I stared at the small, green oilskin packet which he had taken from his pocket and flung down on the kitchen table.

It was Flora who broke the silence. 'I see how it's to be done,' she cried, jumping up.

'It can't be done, Flora,' I told her. 'Not by tonight.'

'Stands to reason,' Nellie agreed.

'Oh, yes it can,' Flora said rather breathlessly. She was pink with excitement. 'Mr Tregarth won't have to take the packet. We will. We'll go to Cornwall on the train, and we shall be with Samuel by tonight. Can't you see?' she finished triumphantly. 'It's the most perfect answer.'

'By thunder, the little lady's right, ma'am,' Joel Tregarth said, crashing his fist down on to the table so that all the crockery rattled. 'Now if you would agree to the two of them travelling down together on the train, and if you were to send a telegram saying they were on their way, why that would solve everything. And what harm could they possibly come to? I can see they're a sensible pair of youngsters. What do you say?'

Nellie had a good deal to say. She said she'd rather go herself than let us travel all that way alone. She said she'd never heard such nonsense in all her life and what was wrong with sending the packet by post? No matter how urgent it was, she said, there was no use telling her that the next morning wouldn't be time enough for it to arrive. She asked Joel Tregarth how he could be so sure that there'd be someone to meet us at the other end if she did send a telegram, and if there wasn't anyone there, what were we supposed to do then, she'd like to know.

Joel Tregarth said that if either Mr Rolandson or Miss Rolandson weren't there to meet us at the station, then he'd eat his hat, and Nellie sniffed and said, 'Very likely,' and 'Fine words butter no parsnips.'

At last Mr Tregarth leaned across the table and tapped the packet. 'If you'll pardon me, ma'am,' he said soberly, 'I must tell you that if Mr Rolandson doesn't receive this packet by tonight he stands to lose a great deal. More than you imagine, I daresay. Of course it's up to you to decide what you think best, but seeing as you set great store by Mr Rolandson, you and the youngsters here, it's only right you should know that you couldn't do him a better service than letting them take this packet down to him on the train.'

'We can't let Samuel down, can we?' Flora pleaded.

'No, we can't,' I agreed. 'And Flora's right. It is the only way.'

'Come now, ma'am,' Joel Tregarth said, looking earnestly at Nellie. 'Say yes, won't you?'

'Oh, all right. 'Ave it yer own way,' Nellie said at last, jabbing a hairpin savagely back into her bun. 'And yer can stop that cavortin' about, Flora, and 'and me the railway timetable from the dresser before I change me mind.'

4. We Set Out

The next two hours were uproar and bobbery, as Nellie would say, for after looking up the timetable we found that the only train to Penzance on a Sunday morning was the Flying Dutchman, which left Paddington Station at half-past ten, so that if we were to deliver the packet to Samuel that evening, we had, somehow, to be on it.

Suddenly there seemed to be a hundred and one things to be thought about and decided upon, and most of them involved running up and down stairs several times. Nellie prided herself on being able to rise to a crisis, on account of her years in the theatre, which, she always said, had been one long crisis from beginning to end, but I wondered whether even she would be able to get us to the station in time to catch the train.

Of course the very first thing that happened was that Flora and Nellie began the usual squabble about what Flora should wear for the journey. Whenever we went anywhere, even out for a walk, there was sure to be an argument about coats, or gloves, or hats. This time is was because Flora wanted to wear her new summer coat and skirt and Nellie wouldn't let her.

'I'll be far too hot in my winter things,' Flora pouted.

Nellie shook her head. ' "Ne'er cast a clout till May is out" and it's only April. Besides it's always colder in the country.'

'What does it matter anyhow?' I said. 'If you're too hot you can take your coat off in the train – that is, if we ever catch it.'

'It matters to me,' Flora sulked.

'Anyway, it's vulgar ter wear yer best things when yer go to the country,' Nellie said, sweeping a pile of clothes off the clothes-horse and going out of the door. Flora considered this for a moment and then followed Nellie upstairs while Joel Tregarth, who was still sitting in our kitchen, gave me a wink. I saw that he understood very well what it was to have a sister and I grinned back at him across the table.

'I can see you've a great deal to do,' he said, 'so I won't hold you up. I'll be on my way.' He slid the packet across the table towards me, but he didn't take his hand off it and he frowned as though last minute doubts were crossing his mind.

'It's all right,' I said. 'Really it is, Mr Tregarth. Flora thinks it's all a bit of a lark, I daresay, but I understand that it's more than a game, and I swear I'll take care of the package and see that our Guardian gets it safe this evening.' I felt a little foolish saying such things, but Joel Tregarth looked very pleased, and smiled and clapped me on the shoulder. Then he said that Samuel must be proud of me, which made me blush.

'I see you're to be trusted,' he went on, standing up, 'so I'll only say two things to you before I go. Don't give that package to anyone but Samuel Rolandson. And don't tell your business to anyone who asks – no matter who they may be. That way everything will be sure to turn out all right.'

I nodded. 'I promise,' I said. 'Although I wish I knew what it was all about.'

Joel Tregarth put his hand on my shoulder. 'Well, that would be betraying a trust,' he said, 'if I was to tell you what I know.' Then he put his cap back on and straightened it with a tug. 'One thing I can say, though. It all began a great time ago, and I hope for Rolandson's sake that this is the end of the story.' Then he held out his huge, brown hand and wished me good-bye and good luck, and said that one day, perhaps, when all this was over, he'd take me out fishing for mackerel.

I waved to him through the window as he climbed the steps, and the last I saw of him were his sea-boots pacing along past the street railings. When I turned back, the kitchen seemed very empty and quiet.

Then Nellie bustled in and wanted to know what I was doing, standing about like a tailor's dummy when there was so much to be done, and where, she asked, had that Joel Tregarth gone? When I told her he'd just left, Nellie said there was still a hundred and one questions she wanted to ask him and she sent me to fetch him back. I ran up the area steps and into the street, but when I reached the corner there was no sign of him.

'Without a word of a lie,' Nellie said when I told her he'd disappeared, 'I don't know as 'ow I can stand another moment of ter-day, and I don't see as 'ow I'll ever get yer on ter that train.' But somehow she did, and at twenty-seven minutes past ten we all three found ourselves running along the platform and looking for an empty, second class carriage on the Flying Dutchman.

The journey from Kennington to Paddington in a hansom cab had taken the better part of an hour. Nellie grumbled all the way about the expense, but it was the only way to get there in time. I wished that everything wasn't such a rush, because what I really wanted to do was to go up to the front of the train and look at the engine before our journey began. We'd never been on an express train before and I was sure the engine must be magnificent, but when we arrived at the platform it was already hissing and letting off steam to be ready to go.

'Come on you two,' Flora called back. 'Can't you see it's nearly half-past ten and we haven't found a carriage yet.'

'Don't lean out of the window, mind,' Nellie was saying as she panted along beside me. She had to shout to make herself heard above the hiss of steam and the hubbub of people shouting and banging doors and running; she was so agitated by it all that the bunch of violets on the brim of her bonnet was bobbing violently about. 'Don't talk to strangers,' she went on, 'and don't lose yer tickets. Now I'm trusting yer not to lose the tickets, William.'

'I won't lose them,' I promised, doing my best to be patient. Nellie had been giving us a string of such instructions ever since we climbed into the cab.

'And look after yer sister,' Nellie went on. 'And mind yer manners when yer meets Miss Rolandson — I don't want 'er ter think yer not well brought up.'

'Here's a second class carriage,' Flora shouted.

'Well I 'ope it's empty,' Nellie said anxiously, 'or got a lady in it.'

'Anyway it'll have to do. The train's going any moment,' I said, nudging Flora to get in.

It was true. The clock above the platform stood at twenty-nine minutes past, and the guard already had the green flag in his hand. Up and down the length of the train, porters were banging doors shut and people were waving goodbye to friends and relations.

''Ere,' Nellie shrieked as we scrambled into the carriage, 'don't forget the picnic basket or yer'll 'ave no lunch.'

I seized it from her and put it on the seat beside our carpet bag just as the porter closed the door.

'We're going!' Flora gasped, 'and we haven't said goodbye. Open the window, William.'

'It's too late,' I said and as I spoke the guard blew his whistle and the train began to move. It started with a great puff of steam and a jerk which threw Flora and me into a heap on the seat, and by the time we had got to our feet again we were just in time to catch a last glimpse of Nellie waving frantically and blowing kisses, her bonnet slightly askew and the bunch of violets dangling over one eye. It was too late now for her to find a respectable middle-aged lady to keep an eye on us; too late for her to put us in charge of the guard, which she had been threatening to do – and the only other person in our carriage was a man, sitting in the corner, the very last person she would have chosen as a travelling companion for us.

'Well that's that,' said Flora as soon as Nellie had disappeared from sight, and she took off her hat and shook her hair over her shoulders. Then she took off her gloves, which she hated wearing, and threw them on to the seat beside the hat. I watched her, and my heart sank, for I saw at once that she was going to show off most horribly and I shouldn't be able to do anything about it.

First of all Flora bounced up and down on the seat and giggled a great deal and made faces at me. I glared at her, and she bounced even harder so that the man in the corner, who was trying to read his newspaper, looked at her and scowled. Flora smiled back at him and fluttered her eyelashes, which made me so embarrassed that I aimed a hard kick at her shins. Only unfortunately I missed. Then she knelt up on the seat and began fiddling about with the buttons on the upholstery, twisting them round and round till I thought they'd come off. When she tired of that she pushed the arm rest up and down, up and down between her and the man in the corner, until at last he gave her such a glare that she moved back into the corner.

As she did so I hissed at her that if she didn't stop showing off I'd tell Nellie as soon as we got back home. She gave me a look, of course, but she sat pretty still for a while after that, just banging the heels of her boots together and making her laces do a little dance. I didn't pay any attention. I just went on looking out of the window.

The trouble with Flora is that when she's in that showing off mood she just doesn't seem to be able to bear it if people aren't looking at her all the time. I suppose it must have something to do with her wanting to go on the stage, because at other times she can be quite sensible. After all, it had been her idea in the first place to take the package to Samuel, and a very fine idea it had been, as long as she didn't go and spoil everything.

I hadn't had a chance to tell her what Joel Tregarth had said before he left about not telling anyone what we were going to Cornwall for, and I was really afraid that if Flora went on trying to attract the attention of the man in the corner he might begin to talk to us and ask questions, in the way that grown-ups have, and I shouldn't be able to stop Flora from telling him everything.

I looked at the man and he certainly didn't look as though he wanted to talk to anyone. He had put his newspaper down, and was slumped right into the corner, turning his bowler hat round and round in his hands, and as he turned the hat round he stuck out his lower lip as though the two movements somehow went together. His hands were small and fat and dirty, and his fingers were blunt with blackened nails.

Samuel has the best hands I've ever seen. They are long and slender, but most of all they're supple and when he moves them they seem almost like people, because they have a kind of life of their own. He keeps them very clean too, and his nails are always short and without a speck of dirt. Because he's a conjuror his hands are very important to him, and because of that and because they're so good to look at, I often notice other people's hands. Nellie's are like monkey's paws, and red and horny with work, and my own are quite good for doing practical things such as carving bits of wood into shapes, which I enjoy, but they're nothing like Samuel's hands. You can't tell with Flora yet; she's not old enough.

By now Flora was trying to make the man look at her, and the more I glared at her to tell her to stop, the worse it made her. She was staring at him so hard that in the end he was sure to look up. At last he did, and I saw that his eyes were black.

'Could you tell us the time please?' Flora asked, smiling at him and not at all put off by the disagreeable way he was looking at her. 'You see, it feels like lunch time but it may not be, and if it isn't and we eat our sandwiches too soon, then we'll be hungry later on.'

The man nodded, but he didn't smile as he pulled a turnip watch from his waistcoat pocket.

'It is ten minutes to noon. Not lunch time yet, I fear,' he said harshly.

'Oh dear,' Flora answered, giving a little pout and swinging her legs. 'And I'm so hungry, too.'

'Then perhaps you'd care for one of these,' he said, putting his watch away and pulling a paper bag from his coat pocket. 'To take the edge off your appetite,' he

49

added, smiling for the first time as he passed the bag to Flora. It was partly because his teeth were all stained and broken that his smile was so nasty, but I think it was more because although he smiled with his mouth, his eyes stayed just the same, gazing watchfully at Flora. If I'd been her I wouldn't have touched the sweets on any account, but it was too late to say anything, for she had already put one of the brown, sticky things into her mouth. When the man passed the bag to me I shook my head. 'They're called Winter Mixture,' he said, looking back to Flora. 'They have an unusual flavour.'

I could tell almost at once by the expression on Flora's face that the sweet tasted as disgusting as it had looked, and to begin with I was pleased because it served her right for showing off so. But then I saw that the man was still watching Flora and that made me feel sorry for her.

It seemed a very long time before the man turned away and looked out of the window. When he did, I handed my handkerchief to Flora so that she could spit the rest of the sweet into it.

When, after a long time, the train reached Bristol, the man got out and walked away up the platform. He had left his luggage in the carriage, though, so we knew he had only gone to the buffet. We had eaten all our sandwiches by then and were beginning to feel hungry again, and Flora suggested going to buy some chocolate buns, but I said that if she did the train would probably go on without her. I was pretty cross because of the way she had been showing off all the way, and I told her that I wouldn't much mind if she was left behind, and what was more that we'd be in real trouble if the man started talking to us and asking us questions, because Joel Tregarth had said we mustn't tell our business to anyone, no matter who they might be.

'It wouldn't matter what he asked,' said Flora, swinging her foot and pouting. 'I'd just make up some story, and he'd never know.'

'That's all very well,' I said seriously, 'but if anything went wrong it would be all your fault. This isn't a game, Flora. It's important.'

Flora didn't like being lectured. 'I don't like that man a bit, anyway,' she said. 'The sweet he gave me was disgusting. I wish we didn't have him in our carriage.'

'Why don't we change carriages?' I suggested suddenly.

'Yes, let's,' said Flora, jumping up quickly and taking hold of our lunch basket and the carpet bag. But it was too late, for at that moment the man came back with two pork pies and a bottle of beer and settled himself down in his corner again, and a moment later the whistle blew and the train steamed slowly out of the station.

The afternoon seemed to last for ever. To begin with, that morning, it had been interesting to look out of the window and see green fields with cows and sheep grazing in them, rivers winding away into the distance and clumps of trees instead of the streets and houses of London. There had been patches of primroses too, and woods full of bluebells, and when the train wound round a curve in the line, we could see the engine right at the front, and the steam blowing backwards towards us from the funnel. But by the middle of the afternoon I was so tired of looking that I didn't want to see another green field as long as I lived, and the sound of the engine and the wheels on the track, which had seemed so thrilling earlier in the day, now seemed tedious and tiresome.

We were glad when the train stopped at Plymouth, and a man with a buffet trolley came to the window so that we could buy some currant buns and a bottle of ginger pop. Just before the train steamed out of Plymouth station a smaller train, which looked like a local one, pulled in and panted to a halt at the opposite platform. Through the window we saw a single passenger alight. She was tall and graceful, and as she drew the veil down from the wide-brimmed hat that she wore, something about her face made me wonder whether I had seen her anywhere before. I was still puzzling over it as the Flying Dutchman picked up speed.

After Plymouth the train stopped often and the stations had weird, unfamiliar names. Liskeard. Bodmin Road. Truro. I wondered what Nellie was doing, in Kennington. The sun slanted lower and lower and filled the carriage, and the train, which had sounded so brisk and business-like that morning, puffed and panted up and down the hills and through the tunnels as though it didn't expect to arrive for at least a week and didn't much care either.

I think that Flora went to sleep first. I remember that her head was on my shoulder and she was hugging the lunch basket as though it was very precious indeed, which it wasn't, being quite empty. The man in the corner had been asleep ever since we pulled out of Plymouth, and had been snoring for some time, with his newspaper covering his face.

When I next woke up the train had stopped. The gas lamp in the carriage roof had been turned on some time while we were asleep, and in its hissing, greenish light I saw that we were alone in the compartment. The man from the corner seat had gone, and so had his luggage. I struggled free of Flora, who was lolling against my shoulder still fast asleep, and opened the carriage door. I could see the sign on the platform which said Penzance, and one or two people who were still straggling towards the barrier. There was no sign of Samuel.

'Come on, Flora. Time to wake up,' I said, shaking her. 'We've arrived.'

She followed me out on to the platform yawning, and still half asleep. I had to take the carpet bag and the lunch basket because she was carrying her hat, dangling it by the strings from one hand. She seemed to have mislaid her gloves altogether and her bootlaces were both undone. 'Where's Samuel?' she asked, between yawns. 'I can't see him. Is he here?'

'Come on,' I told her. 'He's probably waiting by the barrier.'

But Samuel wasn't by the barrier either. We went out into the station yard when I had handed over our tickets, and I was wondering whether Nellie had forgotten to send the telegram and what on earth we should do if there was no one to meet us, when a voice said: 'Are you for Spindrift House? Is your name Rolandson?'

'Yes we are,' I said, and Flora cheered up at once when she saw that the old man who had spoken was holding the reins of a donkey cart.

'You'd best climb on,' he nodded, looking at us kindly and taking the carpet bag from my hand. 'I've been asked to take you both up the hill to Spindrift.'

Flora was so pleased at the prospect of a ride in the donkey cart and of seeing the sea that she hardly seemed to care that Samuel had not come to the station to meet us. I thought it very odd though. 'I'm sure there's a good reason,' Flora said, tucking the rug round us both. 'You'll see.'

As we drove out of the station yard I looked back over my shoulder and saw, standing under the gas lamp and staring after us, the man who had been in our carriage. It was almost as though he was watching us. When I told Flora that, though, she only tossed her head and said that I was silly. 'I expect he's waiting for someone,' she said.

The thing I remember best about that drive is the wind and the smell of the sea. It was a damp, soft wind and it was warm. Before we had left the harbour and the town behind us, our lips were salty and drops of wetness clung to our hair and clothes. We couldn't see very much for it was dark, but we vaguely heard the murmuring of the sea on the shore as the town receded.

Around the harbour there had been a few lights, but now there were none at all and it was quite dark, which felt strange to Flora and me, for we were used to the lighted streets of London. After a while we began to climb a hill.

'Nearly there now,' said the old man over his shoulder and before long he turned the donkey in at a gateway. There was a short, steep drive and in front of us we saw a low house, lit by a lamp that stood in the porch.

Flora tugged at my sleeve. 'When we get inside, will you let me tell Samuel about . . . you know . . .' she whispered, meaning the packet. 'After all, it was my idea to come.'

'Yes,' I said. 'Yes, all right,' but all the time I was wondering why Samuel hadn't heard the donkey cart and come to meet us.

'Don't forget,' Flora said, and jumping down as soon as the cart stopped she ran into the porch, leaving me to follow with the carpet bag and the lunch basket.

The woman who opened the door to us was short and fat with a very flushed red face and a small mouth that turned down at the corners. She was dressed in black. 'I see old Tom found you at the station then,' she said, looking Flora and me up and down in a disapproving way and frowning at the carpet bag and the lunch basket. 'Well, come in then,' she went on, 'since you are here, and give me your damp things.'

'Thank you,' I said, stepping into the hall, 'but first of all, can we please see our Guardian, Samuel Rolandson.'

The woman shook her head so that her fat red cheeks wobbled. 'You've made a mistake,' she said looking from one to the other of us. 'Mr Rolandson isn't here.'

5. Squab Pie and Secrets

'Not here?' I gasped. 'But he must be here.'

'Are you calling me a liar, young fellow?' the woman demanded, going redder than ever and wobbling her cheeks like an angry turkey cock.

'Of course not,' I said, standing my ground. 'But our Guardian left this address and he said he'd be here. So if he's not – well, then – where is he?'

'You can't expect me to know where he is,' she said. 'Mr Rolandson didn't tell me where he was going when he left and it wasn't my place to enquire.'

'So he's been here then?' I said quickly.

'Oh, yes,' the woman said, folding her hands in front of her. 'He's been here all right.'

'Where's our aunt?' Flora asked suddenly, stepping forward and staring up into the woman's red face. 'You're not Miss Rolandson, are you?'

'I certainly am not,' she said, glaring at Flora. 'I'm Mrs Turvey, the housekeeper at Spindrift, and I may as well tell you that I don't like your tone, young madam.'

'I want to see Miss Rolandson,' Flora said obstinately. 'We both want to see her, don't we, William?'

'Well, you can't,' said Mrs Turvey, 'Miss Rolandson's not here either. She's gone to Plymouth on urgent business.'

'I don't believe you,' Flora said rudely. Mrs Turvey gasped.

'Look,' I interrupted, 'I'm afraid you don't understand. Flora doesn't mean to be rude, but we have to see our Guardian as soon as possible. We have to see him tonight. Is there anything you can do to help us find him?'

'I have no idea of Mr Rolandson's whereabouts,' Mrs Turvey said with an air of finality. 'He arrived here this morning, and he left again this afternoon without saying where he was going, and as far as I know he is not expected back at Spindrift.'

'But didn't he get our telegram?' I asked. 'Didn't he even see that?'

'The telegram,' said Mrs Turvey grimly, 'arrived just after Mr Rolandson left.'

Flora and I looked at each other and I saw two tears slide slowly down her cheeks. 'It's hopeless,' she said in a small voice. 'Whatever shall we do? I wish we'd never come.'

'Cheer up,' I whispered. 'It's not that bad.'

'It is,' said Flora with a gulp. 'I wish we were back at home.'

'Yes,' said Mrs Turvey, who had moved a step closer to hear what we were saying, 'and back home is where you're going first thing in the morning. This house is no place for children. What made you come anyway?' she asked, looking from one to the other of us. 'What's this business you've got with Mr Rolandson that's so important?'

I shot Flora a warning glance. Whatever happened I knew we must not say one word to Mrs Turvey. 'It's private,' I muttered. 'It's very private indeed.'

'Huh!' she snorted, her red cheeks wobbling. 'Just as I thought. Some prank I daresay, and only what I'd expect, being brought up the way you have. Well come along then, take off those damp things like I told you to, and come and have your supper since I've gone to the trouble of getting it ready for you. I suppose you want something to eat, don't you?'

'Don't tell her anything, however much she asks,' I whispered to Flora as soon as Mrs Turvey had stumped away across the stone-flagged hallway. 'I don't trust her.'

'Nor do I,' said Flora. 'Do you suppose it's all right to eat? I mean she might put poison in our food. And what are we going to do about the packet?'

'I don't know,' I said, 'but we must have something to eat. I can't think when I'm empty.'

'Well I don't suppose it'll be poisoned,' Flora said, sniffing the delicious smell that was coming from the kitchen. 'It *smells* all right,' and she followed me across the hall.

The kitchen was brightly lit with a pair of oil lamps which hung from hooks on the ceiling and if it had been Samuel standing there, beside the table, instead of Mrs Turvey I daresay we would have thought it the most delightful room in the world. It was long and low with a stone-flagged floor and a huge range, twice the size of ours at home. There was a bright fire burning in the grate and the brass fender shone like gold in the lamplight. Beside the range there was a rocking chair and against the wall was a long dresser covered with rose-patterned china. The scrubbed deal table was set for two and Mrs Turvey was already cutting into the crust of a pie and putting generous helpings on to our plates. The pie was full of bacon and onion and savoury herbs and tasted as good as it smelt, and as I couldn't believe that anything so delicious could possibly be poisoned, I tucked in with a will and so, I noticed, did Flora.

While we were eating, Mrs Turvey sat in the rocking chair with her feet on the fender. She was mending a tear in a blue and white tablecloth and her needle flew in and out, but she never said a word though she looked up at us from time to time. As soon as she saw we had finished she put her sewing aside and stood up.

'Squab pie that is,' she said, coming to the table. 'By rights it should be made with a seagull baked in the middle, but that's the old way.' Then she picked the pie up, carried it out to the larder, and came back a moment later with two candles which she lighted in the flame of the fire and stuck into candlesticks. 'There's no oil lamps on the top landing so you'll need these,' she said, moving towards the door.

'We don't usually go to bed as early as this,' I said, glancing at the kitchen clock. 'It's not nine yet.'

'I daresay,' Mrs Turvey answered, her small mouth growing even smaller with disapproval, 'but we keep regular hours down here.'

Flora and I looked at each other and Flora shrugged. At least if we went up to bed we'd be on our own and we'd be able to talk without her listening to us.

We followed Mrs Turvey out into the hall where she paused for a moment to hand one of the candlesticks to Flora. Then, after picking up a small oil lamp from the chest and motioning me to bring the carpet bag, she led us up the shallow staircase to the very top of the house. Our rooms were next to one another under the eaves. Mrs Turvey put a candle in each room and was about to go back downstairs when I put out my hand and stopped her.

'Please, Mrs Turvey,' I said, 'are you quite sure our Guardian won't be back later tonight?' She shook me off and began to go downstairs. 'Or Miss Rolandson,' I called after her. 'Will she be back?'

She turned and looked back up the stairs at Flora and me standing side by side on the landing and she shook her head. I saw her red cheeks wobbling in the light of the oil lamp. 'By the time Miss Rolandson returns, you'll be in London,' she said, 'and as for your Guardian, I've already told you I've no idea where he is, and as far as I know he's not returning here. You'd best make up your mind to it, young man, you're going back to London by the first train tomorrow, and I hope that'll teach you a lesson.' And with that she stumped off down the stairs, leaving us alone.

We crept into Flora's room and sat on the bed staring at the flickering light of the single candle on the dressing-table. 'What did she mean she hoped it would teach us a lesson?' Flora asked, unlacing her boots and tugging them off.

'She thinks we've come here as some practical joke,' I said wearily, 'just for a lark.'

'I don't think she likes us much,' Flora said after a moment, 'but I don't see why. We haven't done anything wrong. You don't suppose anything dreadful's happened to Samuel do you, William?'

'Of course not,' I said quickly, for the very same thought was in my own mind. 'Samuel's far too clever to let anything go wrong with his plans. It's just a misunderstanding, that's all.'

'And our aunt's not here either,' Flora murmured. 'I'm sure it wouldn't be like this if she was here.'

'The worst thing of all,' I told her, 'is about the packet. I promised faithfully that we'd get it to Samuel by tonight – and now I've broken my promise.'

'That's not your fault,' Flora said quickly. 'Joel Tregarth said Samuel would be here, and Samuel left this address himself.'

'All the same,' I said, standing up and going over to the dressing-table, 'we've failed, haven't we?'

'Oh William,' said Flora miserably, 'what are we going to do?'

'I don't know,' I said, rubbing a gobbet of warm candle grease between my fingers. 'I think we'd better go to bed. Maybe in the morning something will happen.'

'The only thing that'll happen in the morning is that Mrs Turvey will send us back to London,' Flora said, struggling with the buttons down the back of her blouse. After a few moments puffing and straining she put her arms down and said in a hopeless voice, 'You'll have to help me. There are some I just can't reach no matter which way round I go.'

Later when we were both in bed Flora called out, 'Are you still awake?'

'Yes,' I answered.

'Have you put your candle out yet?'

'Yes,' I said. 'Don't worry Flora, if I hear anything in the night I'll come and make sure you're all right.'

'Thank you,' she answered in a small voice. 'I'm going to blow my candle out now, William.'

The last thing I remember is that I clutched the oilskin packet tightly in my hand under the pillow before I went to sleep.

I must have slept particularly well, because I don't remember anything more until I opened my eyes to find the room filled with sunshine and Flora sitting on the end of my bed brushing her hair. As soon as I opened my eyes she leaned forward and began to talk, without even waiting for me to yawn or stretch. Flora is always fearfully bright first thing in the morning.

'I've been all over the house,' she said. 'I've been into every single room. Samuel's not in any of them, and nor is our aunt, but the house is as strange as can be. It's not big, but the rooms are such queer shapes with windows where you least expect them, and the passages are all up and down steps and round corners.

There's one room full of paintings, I suppose it must be a studio because there's an easel there too and paints and brushes and it's got a window in the roof. But the drawing-room is best. There's a piano with a red silk shawl on it and a vase with peacock's feathers and a Chinese cabinet . . . and a window going out into the garden, and in the garden there's a bird bath like a shell and brick paths . . .'

'Flora!' I bawled. 'Be quiet!'

'There's no need to shout,' she said, looking hurt. 'I was only telling you.'

'I'm sorry,' I said, 'but I can't think with you going on and on, and we've got to work out what to do.' I felt for the oilskin packet and pulled it out from under my pillow. 'Is that Mrs Turvey around?'

'Oh, yes,' said Flora. 'She's been up for hours.'

I groaned. 'Well why didn't you wake me up earlier, then?'

'How could you William?' she pouted. 'At home you won't let me wake you however late it is.'

'At home it's different,' I told her. 'And get off my feet.'

Flora climbed off the bed wearing her haughty look and went over to the window where she stood brushing her hair. I lay down again and stared at the ceiling, trying to think. After quite a long silence Flora looked round at me. 'I wish you'd get up,' she said. 'I can see you're not thinking at all and ideas never come when you lie and wait for them. You have to be doing something and then they suddenly pop up. Did you know you can see the sea from here?'

Flora was quite right about having ideas, but I wasn't going to say so. I climbed out of bed all the same, though, and went over to the window. Of course we'd been to the sea before. Samuel used to take rooms each summer at Sandwich Bay.

But it was different. Almost all I could see from the window was a great, shimmering sheet of water. That was because the house stood at the top of the hill and there didn't seem to be anything between us and the sea except a few roofs and the tops of some dark pine trees. It was like being perched up in a high nest.

Below us, across the surface of the water in the bay, the sun was making a liquid silver path towards an island which rose up out of the sea, looking just like a picture from one of Flora's books of fairy stories. Perched right on the top of the island was a turreted castle. The sight of it was so beautiful and magical that it almost took my breath away and I just stood there, staring and staring, and taking deep breaths of the wonderful, fresh morning smell of sun and sea and trees.

It was warm, too, much warmer than it would have been in London, and the sun which shone through the window on to my face was quite hot, although it was still so early. Far out on the silvery water of the bay I could see the brown sails of a fishing boat and I remembered what Joel Tregarth had said about taking me mackerel fishing. I wished that we were going that very morning instead of having to decide what to do about the package and Samuel still not being there. I sighed.

'Isn't the castle beautiful,' Flora said dreamily. 'Suppose we lived there. Suppose we stayed here always and never went back to Kennington. Like a story . . .'

'It's no good going on like this,' I said suddenly. 'We're not thinking at all. We must . . .' I broke off. There were footsteps coming up the stairs and the next moment Mrs Turvey pushed open the door and came in.

'So you're up are you?' she said, banging down a brass can so hard that the hot water slopped over on to the floorboards. 'Well, you can share that between you – and don't take all day getting dressed. Your train leaves at ten o'clock.' I opened my mouth to say something, but she had turned and was off, thumping down the stairs again.

'That horrid woman,' Flora said. 'She doesn't give us a chance to say a word.'

'Don't worry,' I said, thoughtfully pouring half the hot water into the china washing bowl on the stand. 'I mean to tackle her at breakfast. I think she's hiding something. I think she knows more than she says she does.'

'Do you mean she knows where Samuel is all the time?' Flora asked, her eyes growing very round.

'Perhaps,' I said. 'I'm not sure yet. I just feel that something very peculiar is going on.'

Flora nodded. 'That would explain why she wants us out of the way.'

While we were dressing and I was doing up all the little buttons down the back of Flora's blouse we agreed that during breakfast I would talk to Mrs Turvey and ask her questions, while Flora listened and looked round for any hints or clues there might be. Afterwards we'd decide what to do.

As soon as we were dressed Flora said she wanted to show me the studio, so we tiptoed down to the first landing and along the passage towards the room at the end. We had to go very quietly for fear of Mrs Turvey hearing, and although we were careful to walk on the strip of carpet running down the middle of the passage, every floorboard seemed to creak.

'Isn't it lovely,' Flora whispered, pushing the door

open so that I could look in. 'Our aunt must be very clever to do all those paintings.' There was a painting on the easel of a girl about Flora's age holding a bunch of daffodils. 'Do you think,' Flora asked, looking at it wistfully, 'that she'd do one of me?'

'What's through there?' I asked, pointing to a door at the far end of the room.

'Just a bedroom,' Flora shrugged. 'I peeped in, but it's empty.'

'You listen for Mrs Turvey,' I told her. 'I'm going to look.'

'She'll hear us, I know she will,' Flora whispered anxiously as I tiptoed across the studio, 'and there's nothing there.'

'I'll only be a moment,' I said, quietly turning the knob and pushing the door open.

At first I thought Flora was right. The room was very bare, with only a bed, a washstand and a small dressing-table under the window with a chair beside it. In the corner there was a mahogany wardrobe with the door slightly ajar. Then I looked at the bed again. There was a shirt on it, folded and freshly laundered; a white shirt with a thin blue stripe in it, the very same as Samuel wore.

I walked across the room and flung open the wardrobe door. Inside, hanging up, was Samuel's good, dark suit and his travelling cape, and below on the boot rack were his black boots and beside them his travelling bag. Now I knew for certain that Mrs Turvey had been lying to us, for Samuel would never have left his good clothes behind unless he intended to return. But where had he gone? And why?

'William! She's coming!' Flora hissed. 'Quick!'

With a pounding heart I closed the wardrobe and

darted back across the room and into the studio, shutting the bedroom door behind me. I was only just in time, for I could hear Mrs Turvey stumping along the corridor, and the next moment she burst into the studio.

'What are you doing in here?' she demanded, her red cheeks wobbling with fury.

'We were only looking at the paintings,' I said as innocently as I could. 'Isn't that right, Flora?'

'No one's allowed in here. No one!' Mrs Turvey gobbled, seizing Flora roughly by the arm and pushing her towards the door. 'Your aunt would be very angry if she knew you'd been in here.'

'I'm sorry,' I said, 'but the door wasn't locked and we haven't touched anything. It's a pity,' I went on, following them out into the passage and going slowly so that Mrs Turvey could see I wasn't afraid of her, 'that we have to go back to London today. If we stayed till this evening we could meet our aunt.'

'Your aunt won't be back today,' Mrs Turvey said, slamming the studio door shut and locking it.

'I thought you said last night that she would,' I murmured, watching her slip the key into her apron pocket.

'Now don't you contradict me, young man,' Mrs Turvey said furiously. 'She won't be back today, and that's that. You two are going back where you came from on the ten o'clock train. You're not wanted here.'

'We only came for a lark anyway,' I said, winking at Flora so that she would know I didn't mean it, 'so you needn't suppose we care.'

'Ha!' snorted Mrs Turvey triumphantly, 'just as I thought! Well, the donkey cart will be here in half an hour,' she went on, stumping downstairs in front of us, 'and Mrs Pelgelly from up the hill has offered to go to the station with you. You won't get round her in a hurry I can tell you.'

During breakfast I managed to whisper to Flora about Samuel's clothes while Mrs Turvey went to the larder for another pat of butter. 'What are you whispering about now?' she demanded, coming back to the table and glaring at us.

Fortunately she was interrupted by the sound of someone singing a hymn in a rich, deep voice and a moment later we heard footsteps outside, followed by a knock at the back door. Mrs Turvey looked very flustered and didn't seem to know what to do. Then she took Flora's arm and hustled us both out of the room, telling us to go up and pack and look sharp about it because the donkey cart would be here at any moment.

As soon as we got outside Flora took my arm and pulled me farther away from the door. 'If Samuel's things are here that woman has been lying to us,' she said.

'Yes,' I nodded. 'I wonder her tongue hasn't turned black and withered at the root.'

'I'm not going on that train,' she said in a low, fierce voice. 'Samuel's in some kind of danger. I'm sure of it. We must do something, William. We must.'

'If we knew who was at the door it might help us,' I whispered. 'She didn't want us to see him – whoever he was.'

'We can't hear from here,' Flora said, after putting her ear to the door. 'It's too thick. But I've got an idea.' She darted away and I followed her. We went through the drawing-room and out of the long window into the garden and then I saw what Flora meant. The kitchen stuck out a long way at the back of the house and halfway down there was an open window. When we were close we dropped on to our hands and knees and crawled along until we were underneath it. Although the window was only open at the top Mrs Turvey's voice floated out quite clearly.

'Of course they don't know he's here,' she said scornfully, 'and it's a good thing we'd hidden him away before the telegram came yesterday, or there'd have been trouble.'

'A deal of trouble, I daresay,' a man's voice answered, with a chuckle.

'Well here's the things you asked for,' Mrs Turvey's voice went on. 'The food's enough for a couple of days if you don't let him eat too much – and here's the rope.' She paused. 'There's plenty here for six men I'd say.'

'As long as it'll tie one up it'll be enough,' the man growled.

Flora put her hand over her mouth and stared at me in horror. My mind was in a whirl. What on earth had Samuel done that they should be keeping him a prisoner, and where did our aunt fit in?

'Where are the young 'uns now?' the man asked.

'I sent them up to pack. The donkey cart will be here directly, and Mrs Pelgelly is taking them down to the station. They won't get round her.'

'I daresay not,' the man replied. 'What made them come in the first place?'

'Just took it into their heads,' Mrs Turvey answered. 'Quite out of hand they are. The boy in particular. You should have heard how he answered me back, but then, what can you expect after the way they've been brought up . . .' We didn't wait to hear any more. I took Flora's hand and together we ran back into the house, through the beautiful drawing-room and across the hall.

The drive was lined with thick bushes which hid us,

and it was just as well, for before we reached the gate we saw a stout lady dressed in shiny black satin and a purple bonnet making her way up the drive. She didn't see us, and neither did the driver of the donkey cart who passed us a few moments later.

6. Hodge

'Somehow I just can't believe that any of this is really happening,' I panted, after we had run for some distance up the white, dusty road. My heart was thumping and I kept looking back, half expecting to see Mrs Turvey pounding after us. 'Do you suppose it's all a dream?'

'You couldn't dream all that about the clothes, could you?' Flora gasped. I had been holding her hand and pulling her after me, but now she broke away and stopped, bending double in the middle of the road and holding her side.

'What is it?' I asked anxiously.

'Dreadful stitch,' she panted.

'We can't stop here,' I said. 'Someone might come along.' I looked up and down the road. 'Look!' I pointed. 'There's a wood a little way along. We can hide in there. It's not far.' We ran on until we reached the place and then plunged under the trees.

It was quite a small wood. We could see at once where it ended, and beyond it was a green field rising up to the brow of a hill. The trees were tall and grey-green with age. Lichen covered their branches and their slender trunks like a furry jacket. Between the trees on the ground there were patches of small white flowers, which Flora said reminded her of stars, and moss and grass. There were no bushes, but as we looked around for somewhere to hide we saw, scattered here and there through the wood, huge, irregular shaped boulders which looked as though they had been flung down by some giant in bygone times, so that they had come to rest higgledy-piggledy and had stayed there ever since. One, especially large and covered with moss, was certainly big enough to hide us from view and I pulled Flora down behind it.

For a minute or two we just sat, trying to catch our breath. I leaned my back against the hard, cool stone of the boulder and looked up at the crazy branches of the old trees. I could see blue sky through them, but the sun seemed to have been left behind on the road.

At first it was very quiet and then a little breeze ran through the wood and the branches knocked together and creaked. A huge bird, black as soot, landed on one of the trees cawing so loudly that both Flora and I jumped and Flora gave a little scream.

'It's only a bird,' I said. 'Are you scared?'

Flora nodded. 'Aren't you? Mrs Turvey must have found out by now that we've gone. She's sure to come after us.'

'She won't know where to look though,' I grinned. 'We might have gone down into the town instead of coming up here, and there was a fork in the road farther back. Besides she'll search all over the house and the garden first and that will take a long time.'

'All the same,' Flora said, 'she might quite easily find us you know. We mustn't stay here too long now that my stitch is better.'

'We don't know what we're going to do yet,' I said. All we had known as we ran down the drive was that we weren't going to let Mrs Turvey put us on the train back to London, but we were in a strange place and we had no one to turn to for help. I dug gloomily at the ground with a bit of stick.

'We do know what we're going to do,' said Flora.

'We're going to find Samuel.' She said it in a very matter-of-fact, cool way, as though there would be no difficulty about it at all.

'And where do you think we should start our search?' I asked her. She was silent. 'You see,' I said. 'You don't even know where to begin, do you?'

'That doesn't matter,' Flora answered, shaking her head. 'What matters is that however frightened we may be, we mean to do it. And we do, don't we?'

'I suppose so,' I muttered, after a pause.

'It's not only the package now,' Flora went on. 'Samuel's in some dreadful danger – I just know he is, and because of that I know that somehow we'll find a way to get to him.' It didn't sound a bit like Flora speaking. I knew that she could be quite sensible some-times, but this was different and I looked at her in real surprise. She gave a little smile. 'You're thinking that I'm not being like me at all, aren't you? You're sensible all the time, you see, and I know you think I'm a fearful show-off and silly, but I don't have to be like that. I can be sensible too, when it's really im-portant, and underneath there's quite a different, grown-up kind of me, just waiting for the right moment to show what I can do.' She looked at me defiantly, and I could see she was frightened that I would laugh at her.

'I'm silly sometimes too,' I said and threw the bit of stick towards the nearest tree. Flora smiled at me and clasped her hands tightly together. 'We must both think very hard about how we can find Samuel,' she said.

That was all very well, but after quite a long silence we both of us had to admit that we hadn't any idea of where to begin. Flora suggested that we ought to walk on until we found a police station and then go inside and ask for help, but I said I didn't think that was at all a good idea. After all, the police are like all grown-ups and probably wouldn't believe what we told them, which would be sure to sound pretty much as though we'd made it up for a lark; they might even take us back to Mrs Turvey.

Then I pulled the package out of my pocket and we both looked at it. I suggested that we ought to open it, because it might help us to find Samuel if we knew what was inside. Flora said we ought not to, and if I did she would close her eyes and not look because she thought it was wrong. That made me cross, so I said that if she was such a little angel, perhaps she'd care to think of a better idea, and she said she couldn't think of anything else at all, so we'd better pray for a miracle.

After that we didn't talk for some time. I picked the moss off the boulder with my finger nail and Flora picked a bunch of the white flowers. And then a miracle did happen, though at first it didn't seem like one.

'As pants the hart for cooling streams, When heated in the chase,' the voice was singing as it approached, closer each moment, along the road.

'It's the man who came to the door,' Flora mouthed, her eyes very wide. I nodded, feeling my heart begin to drum. There was nothing to be done except to crouch close behind the boulder, and wait.

'So longs my soul, O God, for thee, And thy refre-e-eshing grace . . .' He was so close when he stopped singing that we could hear his footsteps on the road, and I felt sick with fright. It was like playing hide-and-seek in a dark house, wondering whether he would find us or not. But it wasn't a game. It was real. Flora had stuffed her fingers into her ears, and the bunch of flowers she had picked lay scattered on the ground.

'Jerusalem the Golden,' the voice began again, plain-

73

tively this time. 'With milk and honey blessed. Beneath thy contemplation . . .' He broke off and hummed the rest of the line. The footsteps did not falter. They passed us and grew fainter, and the sound of the hymn faded and then came back, carried on the breeze, but still fading.

Suddenly it was as clear as day what we had to do. I waited a moment or two longer, and then pulled Flora's hands away from her ears. 'Gone!' I said quietly. Then I stood up. 'Come on,' I told her. 'We're going after him.'

'But he's looking for us,' Flora exclaimed, staring at me as though I'd gone mad.

'I don't think he is,' I said. 'You don't walk as quickly as that if you're looking for somebody. And you don't sing either. You listen. I think he's on his way back to the place where they're keeping Samuel prisoner, with the food and the rope. If we follow him . . .'

'He'll see us, though,' Flora said, looking doubtful, but standing up and brushing the twigs off her skirt.

'Not if we're careful.' I felt excited. 'Don't you see? It's the miracle we wanted.'

Flora looked at me, and then she nodded. 'All right,' she said. 'I'm ready.'

We went cautiously through the wood and out again on to the road. In the distance we could see the solitary, plodding figure of the man. There was no one else in sight.

All at once I felt that everything might turn out all right. I laid my hand on my heart, feeling the lumpy oilskin packet in my inside pocket and turned to Flora. ' "And so Sir Hubert and his gallant young page Florizel set off in search of the Knight of the White Dove" – that's Samuel,' I added with a grin.

74

'Supposing he turns round?' Flora asked, pointing to the man ahead of us on the road.

'He won't,' I said, 'and if he does he won't see who we are so long as we don't get too close to him. Don't you want to be Florizel?'

'It's too important for games,' Flora said, looking at her boots.

The road ran straight at first, but before long it began to twist between tall, green banks where gorse bushes and heather and wild flowers grew. The banks were too high for us to be able to see over the top, but when we passed gateways into the fields we could see farm-houses and cattle grazing and more fields which made a distant patchwork.

Above us the sky was blue and clear. The sun beat down upon us and before we had gone very far we felt hot and tired and wished that we could sit down on the grass, but the man ahead of us kept on walking. His pace did not slacken and he didn't look round. Every so often we heard the snatch of a hymn tune, but otherwise there was only the song of a bird far up in the sky and the breeze in the gorse. We saw no other human being. Cattle looked up as we passed and gazed at us through the bars of their gates, but cattle are not people.

Flora and I were not used to so much silence and it wasn't possible to be lonely in Kennington. I began to feel that the whole thing was a dream, the trudging figure in front of us some nameless creature from a nightmare who never went farther away nor came closer. The road, too, was full of potholes and stones large enough to stumble over and twist one's ankle. Before long our boots were white with dust and it seemed to settle in our throats and in our hair and eyes. Flora began to grumble about how hot her clothes were.

'Just think about Samuel,' I told her, wiping my hand across my forehead and wishing the sun were not quite so bright.

'I'm trying to. But I'm getting a blister on my heel. If it gets really bad I shan't be able to walk. What shall we do then?' I didn't answer.

To our right the land had become wilder now. Rough open moorland climbed to the skyline, studded with the same huge boulders that we had seen in the wood. Here and there, tall stones reared up like sentinels standing guard. A little farther along we came upon a reed-fringed pool which stood by the side of the road. Flora was for stopping and bathing her face and hands, but when we came closer we saw that all around the pool there was thick, wet mud where the cows had trodden a path to drink, and there was no way for us to reach the water.

We went on. The road suddenly made a sharp bend and, as we came round the corner, there, sitting with his back to a milestone where two roads met, was the man. He was only a few yards away from us, but his head was turned or he would certainly have seen Flora and me. We walked backwards, cautiously until he was hidden from our view again, and then we scrambled up the bank on the left-hand side of the road and dropped down into the grass field amongst the daisies. From there we could hear the man muttering to himself, and then a pause, after which he smacked his lips as though he had been drinking.

I signalled to Flora to stay where she was and crawled on a little farther, edging myself up the bank behind the shelter of an overhanging thorn bush. I had stopped worrying about whether my jacket and trousers got dirty and I crawled on my stomach, very slowly until I reached the top of the bank. From there

I was able to look down on the man directly below me.

I could see the red and white spotted handkerchief he had spread on his knees, and the bread and cheese he was eating for his lunch. He wore brown leather gaiters and boots and his legs stuck straight out in front of him. He had a striped woollen hat on his head, and the red bobble moved a little as he cut the bread. But apart from that, and some grey, bushy whiskers, I could see nothing of his face. Beside him on the ground there was a tray, laid out with bootlaces, ribbons and sweets. There were pins, too, and small books and many other things and I realized that the man was a pedlar.

I was just about to crawl back to Flora and tell her what I had discovered when the man spoke. 'A fine day Jinnifer Tregadgwith,' he said, quite loudly, so that I jumped nearly out of my skin.

'A find day indeed, Hodge. And where be you a' goin'?' said another voice. After a moment I saw a woman coming across the road from the farmhouse beyond the cross roads, holding a tiny child by the hand.

'I'm goin' down to Boscaswell today. For tes the last day of the month and they miners do get paid today,' said the pedlar with a chuckle.

'Well, an' before you go, p'raps you'd have a blue ribbon for my Lizabeth Ann in your pack,' said the woman, pulling her purse from her pocket.

By now Flora was pulling at my boot heels so hard that I had to slide backwards down the bank and tell her what I had seen and heard. By the time I crawled back to my look-out post the woman had gone, and the man was shouldering his pack. I watched him start off, and saw that he was taking the road which led away to the right across the moor. There was no cover for us anywhere along that road, and I slid down and told Flora that we should have to wait until he had reached the brow of the hill before it would be safe for us to follow him. Then we would have to run.

'I'm so thirsty,' Flora said, 'and my blister's very sore.'

'I'm thirsty too,' I said. 'Perhaps we'll come to a stream in a little while, and if we do then you can bathe your feet in it as well.'

'Lovely cold water,' said Flora, closing her eyes dreamily.

'Here,' I said. 'Try a piece of grass.' We climbed up on to the bank and sat on the top, chewing the long, juicy stems and watching the figure of the pedlar, Hodge, grow smaller and smaller. Even if he did look round now, we decided, he'd only think we were a bush or a cow. 'It's safe to go now,' I said at last. 'Are you ready?'

Flora nodded and we slithered down the bank and were back on the road. As we ran towards the right-hand fork, the man dropped down below the brow of the hill and was lost to our sight. We ran until we were as hot as we had been before and even more breathless. Our clothes stuck to our backs and our sides ached. When we couldn't run any more we slowed down to a walk, and then Flora began to limp because of her blister.

At last we reached the brow of the hill, and saw before us a strange and different landscape. There were no more farmhouses or cattle or green fields. Here it was all moorland, rough and brown, patched here and there with yellow gorse bushes, and what houses there were looked more grey than white. But the oddest thing of all were the tall, brown towers which we could see, stuck up like fingers from the land, pointing towards the sky and each one belching out black smoke.

'What are they?' Flora gasped, pointing.

I shook my head. 'They look like chimneys,' I muttered.

'And look! There's a wheel on that one. A huge black wheel.'

'Hodge the pedlar said something about miners,' I said, remembering. 'Perhaps they're mine chimneys.'

'The man!' Flora cried suddenly. 'The pedlar – where is he? We've lost him ...'

'Oh, no,' I muttered, shielding the sun from my eyes with my hand and trying to see a movement on the road ahead. He must have left the road though, for there was no sign of him. My heart sank. To have come so far, and then at the end to be outwitted. 'Can you see anything, Flora?' I asked, desperately.

'No,' Flora said, shaking her head. 'Unless . . . Yes, I can!'

'Where?'

'There – where that row of cottages is. Do you see?'

'I can see someone pegging out washing,' I said.

'Farther along, out on the moor, there's a track and someone moving along it.'

I followed the direction of Flora's finger and sure enough in the distance, a figure was making its way across the moorland in the direction of an isolated cottage. 'That's where he's going,' I said. 'That cottage all on its own. Quick. Whatever happens we mustn't lose sight of him now.'

After a while we came to a track leading off to the right. We had almost reached the line of grey cottages so we knew that it must be the track the pedlar had taken. As we turned up it, Flora slumped down on the grass verge. 'I'm not going another step in these boots,' she said, beginning to unlace them.

'But Flora,' I protested. 'We can't stop now.'

'Look,' said Flora, taking off her stocking.

Then I felt sorry, for her heel was so red and sore and I knew that I couldn't have gone half so far with a blister that size. I pulled out my handkerchief and made it into a bandage and helped her to tie it round her foot. Then I said I thought she'd been pretty brave, and she gave a huge sigh and said hadn't we better go on again. So we did. Flora held her boots by the laces and picked her way along the path quite quickly, but by then the man had disappeared.

We followed the track all the same, and the cottage came closer and closer until we arrived at the place where I thought the pedlar had climbed the wall. There was a field of rough, cropped grass and at the end of it the cottage stood. It was low and grey with small windows and it had a lonely look. No trees grew nearby and there was no garden.

We crouched down behind the wall and looked and wondered what to do next. Then we saw the back door open and Hodge the pedlar come out. He had a jug in his hand and he went towards the rainwater butt and dipped the jug into it. I could make out the blue and red stripes of his hat. It seemed hard to believe that just a field away from us Samuel was being kept prisoner. I wondered whether Hodge had used the rope yet to tie him up. He went back inside the cottage without looking in our direction.

I had just opened my mouth to say to Flora that now we knew where Samuel was, when a voice close behind us said, 'Well, well. If it isn't my two little friends from the train. And what, I wonder, are you doing up here?'

7. Rabbit Stew

It was the man who had shared our railway carriage the day before! He stood, leaning on a walking stick, showing all his stained and broken teeth as he smiled down at us. I was so astounded at seeing him just when we had thought ourselves quite alone, that I stared back at him without being able to think of anything to say.

But Flora was even more surprised than I was, I think, so that she overbalanced and landed on a patch of gorse which must have been painful. 'How dare you creep up like that and give us such a fright?' she demanded angrily, rubbing her behind and frowning as she scrambled off the gorse.

The man was amused. He chuckled and gave a little bow. 'My apologies,' he said in mock politeness. 'I'm sure I never intended to startle you. I may say that I was quite surprised myself to see you both again so soon. I had not expected that I should have the pleasure of meeting you again – and in such an unlikely place.' He waved his stick at the moorland, but he was still staring at us with dark, empty eyes. 'Perhaps,' he went on, 'you will allow me to help you up,' and he held out his hand to Flora.

'No, thank you,' she said crossly. 'We're resting,' and without looking at him she went on trying to take a gorse prickle out of the palm of her hand.

'Ah,' he nodded. 'I see.' He looked at me then, and I looked at the ground not wanting to talk to him or meet his gaze, but he didn't speak and he didn't move.

I wished that he would go away and stop staring at us. He was making me feel uncomfortable and I realized all at once what a sorry sight we must look. Flora's hair was full of tangles and her blouse and skirt were crumpled. She had no stockings or boots on and there were dirty marks on her face. I daresay I didn't look much better myself. 'It seems very near dinner time to find you in such an out of the way spot,' the man said at last. 'Have you lost your way by any chance?'

'Oh, no,' I said at once. 'We're not lost. Not at all.'

'Perhaps you were looking for someone?' he suggested.

'No,' Flora said, removing the prickle at last and brushing the palms of her hands together in a casual way. 'Just out for a walk.'

The man smiled slowly. Then he pulled out his silk handkerchief, shook it, spread it out upon the grass and sat down on it. 'The ground is very damp at this time of the year,' he explained as Flora and I looked at each other in consternation, 'but for England I suppose the weather is good enough. I had forgotten it could be so warm in April.' He laid his walking stick on the grass beside him and regarded us both again. 'Since we have met like this,' he said after a pause, 'allow me to introduce myself. My name is Fennel. Eli Fennel, tin miner – lately of this parish, but now only visiting.' A strange look appeared for a moment on his round, red face and he looked away from us at the moorland. 'Yes,' he murmured. 'Only visiting.' Then he gave a laugh.

He seemed friendly enough and I thought that he was only sorry for us, seeing how tired and bedraggled we looked. But all the same something inside me kept nudging me to stand up and walk away. I didn't like the way he looked at us. I didn't like his smile, or his

82

eyes, or his square, grubby hands. I didn't like his name either. I remembered the way I had seen him watching as we left the station in the donkey cart and I thought it decidedly odd that he should come on us up here, so close to the cottage where Samuel was being kept prisoner. It was probably all coincidence, of course, and if so many strange and unaccountable things had not happened to us since Joel Tregarth delivered the first letter to Samuel I daresay I should have thought nothing of it.

But Flora must have found it odd as well, for she suddenly jumped up. 'Come on William,' she said bossily. 'We've rested long enough,' and she set off up the track, the way we had come, swinging her boots by the laces.

Eli Fennel winked at me and asked whether Flora ordered me about like that all the time and I grinned in a rather sickly way and stood up, brushing the grass off my knees and not quite knowing what to say. I could see that Flora wasn't going to wait for me anyway, because she was walking quite quickly up the track without looking back.

'Well – goodbye,' I said, starting off after her. 'I'd better go.'

Eli Fennel caught up with us almost at once. 'Forgive me,' he said, smiling, 'but are you sure you're not lost?'

'We're not lost at all,' Flora said, shaking her head vigorously. 'We're staying with our Aunt at Five Trees Farm, and we know just how to get back there, thank you. As a matter of fact I have a very good sense of direction,' she added.

'That's all right then,' he said, continuing to walk along beside us. 'For a moment, you see, I thought you were lost but didn't want to admit it. And then I thought that perhaps you didn't want to talk to me because I was a shade disagreeable on the train yesterday.' Flora and I glanced at each other but neither of us answered him. 'Yes,' Eli Fennel chuckled, 'I was as sour as a crab, wasn't I? But then I'd been travelling a long time before I even boarded the train, and to tell you the truth I had a most intolerable headache. But a night of the good sea air of Cornwall has done me a power of good and I feel a new man today.' He smiled at us then, and looked down with concern at Flora's foot. 'I do hope it's not far to your aunt's farm,' he said. 'I see that you've hurt your foot.'

'I haven't exactly hurt it,' Flora said. 'It's a blister, and it's all right now that William's put a bandage on it for me.'

Eli Fennel nodded. 'But what will you do when you reach the road?' he asked. 'It will be hard going without your boots on. I daresay you're not used to walking barefoot and the stones will hurt your feet I'm afraid.'

'She'll put her boots back on again,' I said. 'It's not a bad blister is it, Flora?'

'Cruel brother,' Eli Fennel said, winking at Flora. 'If he had a blister on his foot it would be a different story, eh?'

Flora nodded. 'It *is* rather sore,' she said.

'I'm sure it is,' he said sympathetically. Then he stopped suddenly in the path and banged his stick on the ground. 'Of course,' he said. 'The very thing. My cottage is just over there . . .' He pointed towards the row of cottages where we had seen the woman pegging out washing. 'If you wouldn't mind coming back with me, then I am sure I could find you a sticking plaster. It would be better to put your boots back on again before you walk home and I feel sure a sticking plaster would help. Perhaps you would like a drink as well — you both look thirsty.' He looked from one to the other of us as he spoke.

'It's very kind of you,' Flora said. 'If you're sure it won't be any trouble.'

'No trouble at all I assure you,' Eli Fennel replied. 'You can sit in the shade in the front garden and have a drink while I find the plaster. You know, I think it was a lucky chance that I found you both – just in time eh?' He gave another chuckle, and looked amiably at us. I could see that he was doing his best to be friendly. What harm could we possibly come to, I thought, so long as we stayed in the garden? We should get along much more quickly once Flora had a plaster on her foot and we had both had a drink.

As we walked along, Eli Fennel pointed things out to us in the surrounding landscape. The tall towers that we had thought were to do with coal mines were the engine houses of tin mines, he said.

'Over there,' he went on, stopping and pointing towards a distant brown chimney down on the cliffs, 'that's Boscaswell, the mine where I stared to work when I was a boy. Only thirteen I was. Not much older than you eh? And over there,' he swung round and pointed to a distant chimney on the horizon, beyond the grey cottage, maybe five miles away. 'That one goes by the name of Ding Dong. It's not worked any more; closed down when I was a lad and that's a shame, because they do say that it's been yielding tin since before the time of Jesus Christ. But it's disused now. Deserted. A place where no one ever goes.'

We reached the garden gate of the cottage and Eli Fennel stood aside to let us go in front of him up the brick path. Beyond the porch we could see the dark inside of the cottage, for the front door stood open. Outside there was a rickety green wooden bench set against the wall and shaded by the rambling plant that grew up the front of the cottage. Eli Fennel told us to sit and wait there and he would bring us out some water. I sat down quickly in case he should change his mind and ask us to go inside instead.

'He's quite kind really, isn't he?' Flora whispered, as soon as he had gone inside the cottage. 'I mean he's not at all what I thought he was when we were on the train with him.'

I still wasn't quite certain and I was going to tell Flora to be careful and not ~o start showing off, but Eli Fennel bobbed back again at that moment, carrying a pitcher and a mug. In his other hand he had a shallow china basin for Flora to bathe her feet in. He stood and watched while we drank thirstily, and then he poured some water into the basin and set it down on the ground at Flora's feet.

'There's a delicious smell coming from your cottage,' said Flora when she had bathed her feet and was rubbing them up and down on the grass to dry them. 'What is it?'

'It's a rabbit stew,' Eli Fennel answered, positively beaming at her. 'I made it myself and very tasty it looks.'

'Mm,' Flora crooned, closing her eyes and sniffing. 'It smells tasty too.'

'Now I believe you two are hungry,' Eli Fennel chuckled. 'We're just about to sit down, my old father and I. What do you say to joining us? A plate of good rabbit stew wouldn't come amiss before you walk back I daresay, and you're more than welcome.'

'I'm not sure whether we ought to,' Flora said, giving me a pleading look. 'What do you think William?'

I felt almost as sorry for Flora as I did for myself, because I was absolutely hollow with hunger and goodness only knew when we would be able to eat again, but I stood up. 'I think we'd better go,' I said. 'Thank you very much all the same.'

Eli Fennel looked at me with his head a little on one side. Then he turned to Flora, who I could see was glaring at me in fury.

'Do you know,' he chuckled, 'I have the strangest notion that your brother doesn't trust me. I don't believe that he wants to come inside my cottage. I think . . .' He laughed again. 'I think he must imagine that I mean you some harm. Now why should that be?'

'Oh, pooh!' said Flora jumping up. 'You never can tell with William. He's always imagining the most dreadful things – you've no idea.' Because Flora's foot wasn't hurting any more and she wasn't thirsty or frightened, all her common sense had gone and she was beginning to show off again.

'Come on Flora,' I said, making a grab for her wrist and glaring at her. She dodged away from me.

'The truth of the matter is,' she went on, smiling up at Eli Fennel, 'William threw our lunch to the cows. We had a quarrel, you see, and he got angry; so now we shan't have anything to eat till supper.'

'What a shocking thing to do,' Eli Fennel said, looking at me and speaking in a solemn voice. I felt myself go scarlet with anger and confusion and I glowered at Flora, but there wasn't very much I could say.

'Yes, wasn't it,' Flora said complacently. 'So now we haven't got any lunch you see.'

'Well, that settles it,' Eli said. 'You shall have some stew at any rate. And what about William? Shall we give him some as well do you think?'

'I think so,' Flora said, regarding me slowly. 'He's not always as horrid as that, you see.'

To begin with I was so furious that for two pins I would have walked off and left Flora on her own, which I felt would have served her right. But then I didn't see why I should go hungry while she ate rabbit stew, and I began to reflect that the story she had made up, while not being very flattering to me, *could* have been true and would at least earn us a good, hot dinner. Directly we had eaten Eli Fennel's stew we could be on our way, and there would be no harm done. In the end I followed them inside the cottage.

'You see,' said Eli Fennel to Flora, clapping his hands together and beaming when he saw me. 'I told you the rattle of plates would bring him in. Come on then, Billy boy, for so I shall call you, come and sit down with us.' He waved me to the chair opposite Flora and set a plate of stew in front of me.

Sitting at the end of the table was an old man with untidy white hair and a wrinkled face. He must have been Eli Fennel's father, but the two did not speak to each other and, apart from glancing at Flora and me in surprise from time to time and shaking his head, the old man gave all his attention to his food. He ate the stew quickly and greedily, leaning over his plate and pausing only to spit out the bones. As soon as he had finished, he scraped back his chair, mumbled some words that I couldn't catch and shuffled over towards the front door. A moment later we saw him through the window, lowering himself on to the bench.

'You must forgive the old man,' Eli Fennel said when he had gone. 'He lives alone and he isn't very sociable nowadays. He still enjoys his food though – see how clean his plate is. Now many's the time, in the jungles and mountains of Bolivia, that I've dreamed of coming home to a stew like this. I've been all round the world and eaten many things, both good and bad, but I've never enjoyed a dish so much as this one. Why,' he glanced across at me, running a piece of bread round his plate to gather up the last of the gravy, 'you could set this before a King – or a Zulu warrior chief, eh, Billy boy, and not be ashamed of it. What do you say?'

'It was very good indeed,' Flora said.

'Yes,' I said. 'Very.' Now that I had finished eating I wished that I was outside again in the fresh air, for there was a stale smell of damp earth and rotting sacks in the cottage and the room was dark and gloomy. One of the chair backs was broken and there were crumbs and bits of bacon rind on the table. Cobwebs hung from the ceiling and across the corner of the window.

'Not so fast, not so fast,' Eli Fennel said as Flora stood up. 'We haven't put a plaster on that heel yet, have we?'

'It's much better,' said Flora.

'Nonsense, nonsense. I promised you a sticking plaster – and a sticking plaster you shall have.' He pushed back his chair but didn't get up. Instead he looked from one to the other of us and belched loudly, putting his hand over his mouth too late. 'Just give me a moment to digest,' he went on, 'and then I'll go upstairs and find it. I can see you're anxious to be on your way to Five Trees Farm. I promise I won't hold you up, but sit down for a moment. Yes,' he said, thoughtfully eyeing Flora as she slid back into her chair. 'I've travelled all over the world. Started my mining life in Boscaswell, as I told you, and then, when work was hard to come by I took a ship to Africa. Plenty of mining work there was in those days, but no tin in Africa. It was gold there. Gold and diamonds.' He paused. 'But it wasn't all cake I can tell you. There were Zulus, as black as your hat, with gigantic feathered headdresses and spears. None too pleased to see the white man running over his territory either. Still –

that's all past now.'

The room suddenly seemed very quiet and I felt a prickling up and down my back. I looked at the table.

'Well, well, I can see that all that is of no interest to either of you,' Eli Fennel went on at last, 'and why should it be? I don't suppose you ever met anyone who'd been to Africa before, did you?' He didn't wait for an answer. 'Mind you, not all those who went out there came back. I was once in a party that was attacked by Zulus. There were nearly a hundred of us travelling, and do you know how many survived? Three! Imagine that! Two men and a tiny baby. Just the three of us.'

I could hear him breathing and see the congealed fat round a bit of bacon rind on the table. But I didn't seem able to move. 'Still, as I said, all that's long past. I've made my fortune now I believe, and I'm ready to settle down. Not in England, though. There's a little farm out in Bolivia that I'm going to buy and I'm off there in the morning. Why? What's up boy?' he asked, for I pushed back my chair at last and was standing up.

'Thank you very much for the stew,' I stammered. 'Come on, Flora.'

'No!' Eli Fennel said, jumping to his feet and grabbing my arm. 'We're going upstairs to fetch that plaster first.'

I felt the iron grip of his hand on my arm as he spun me round to face the door which led to the upper floor of the cottage. I tried to tell Flora to run, but it was too late. His arm shot out, and he held her by the wrist.

'You too, Miss Flora,' he smiled. The stairs rose before us, narrow and uncarpeted. 'In the morning I shall be gone,' he continued, as he steered us towards them. 'My business here is nearly over and I shall be taking ship for the port of Rotterdam. But in the meantime I daresay that the safest place for you two will be in here – out of harm's way.' By now we had reached the top of the stairs and he pushed us both into the room at the right. 'I suppose you thought you were deceiving me,' he chuckled. 'You nearly did, you acted so innocent. It was cunning of Samuel Rolandson to use you to do his spying for him, but you've got to be cleverer than a wagonload of monkeys to catch Eli Fennel you know.' He gave a final, harsh chuckle and slammed the door shut. We heard the key turn in the lock.

8. Through the Window

Eli Fennel thumped down the steep flight of stairs and we heard the door close behind him with a squeak and a click when he reached the bottom. We were alone.

I looked at Flora and saw that she had begun to cry. 'Don't!' I begged her. 'Please don't.'

'I can't help it,' Flora sobbed, putting her hands over her face. 'It's all my fault, isn't it? It's because I was showing off again.' I put my arm round her and she looked up at me. 'My story about you throwing our lunch to the cows – he didn't believe any of it, did he?'

'I don't think so,' I said.

'Or Five Trees Farm – he didn't believe that either . . .'

'No,' I said, shaking my head sadly.

'Oh Wil-Wil-William,' Flora gulped. 'What shall we do? I don't understand what's happening any more. He said we were spying on him, but we weren't were we? I want to go home. I wish we'd never said we'd take the horrid packet in the first place, and I wish we'd never come. He's no right to lock us up in here.'

'It'll be all right, Flora,' I said, wanting to comfort her, but not knowing in the least how to do it. 'Really it will. We wanted a miracle before, in the wood, and it came. Perhaps we'll get another one now. But you must stop crying so that we can think. Please, please stop.'

'What's the use of thinking?' Flora hiccupped. 'It won't do any good.'

'Yes it will,' I told her. 'Things aren't as bad as you

imagine. We're not hungry any more for one thing, and we're not thirsty either. We've found out where they're keeping Samuel prisoner – and you've got your boots with you.' I pointed to them lying on the floor and grinned at her. 'It's lucky you brought them, because now you'll be able to run and run without getting prickles in your feet.'

'Don't be silly, William,' Flora answered, half laughing and half crying still. 'We're locked in, aren't we? How are we going to run when we're locked in here?'

'Oh that's easy,' I said, 'because I mean to escape.'

'But how?' Flora asked.

'There's sure to be a way if we only think,' I said airily, 'but you mustn't cry any more because that just wastes time and doesn't do any good.'

'I promise I won't then,' Flora said with unusual meekness. She pulled out her handkerchief and blew her nose energetically while I nodded my approval and then we looked round our prison properly.

It wasn't a very encouraging sight. The room was small and stuffy and it only had three pieces of furniture in it. There was a washstand with a jug and basin on it, a rickety chair and a bed. There was dust everywhere and the room didn't look as though it had been used for a long time; the bed must have been slept in quite recently, however, because it was untidily made with coarse, grey blankets. Flora said that probably Eli Fennel was sleeping in here because the other room, which we hadn't seen inside, belong to his old father.

Above the bed hung a framed text. Flora wiped the dust off it with her handkerchief and read, ' "By the waters of Babylon we sat down and wept." It's done in cross stitch,' she added. A beam of sunlight filtered through the window and made a little golden pool on the dusty boards. The window itself was grimy with dirt and festooned with cobwebs. As we looked a huge spider hurried busily to the centre of its web where a fly buzzed helplessly. Flora shuddered.

I knew that the door was locked, but I couldn't help trying it all the same. 'It wouldn't be any good anyway,' Flora said as I turned back. 'There's only one way out at the bottom of the stairs and he'd only catch us and bring us up here again.'

I paced up and down, trying to think and Flora sat on the ground watching me. 'There must be a way of escaping from here,' I said, 'if only we could think of it.'

'But I can't think,' Flora cried in sudden passion, beginning to beat her clenched fists up and down on the boards so that clouds of dust rose up from them. 'I only know that I hate it in here and I want to get out.'

'I know,' I said, squatting down in front of her and seizing her hands. I didn't want Eli Fennel to hear us in case he came upstairs to see what the noise was about. 'Don't you see,' I went on, 'being here alone gives us a chance to think and work things out, and that's a good thing because if we do escape we shan't have time to do anything except run.'

'But what is there to think about?' Flora asked, calming down and looking at me with a frown.

'A lot,' I told her. 'We know so much more now. We know that Eli Fennel is the reason that Samuel came to Cornwall, and we know that they were in Africa together a long time ago.'

'Yes,' Flora nodded, 'because of what he was saying about the Zulus. That was a trap, wasn't it? To see how much we knew?'

'Yes,' I said.

'It was horrible,' Flora whispered. 'I don't know how I could ever have thought that he was kind. I should have known we couldn't trust him.'

'It's all right,' I said. 'It's not your fault, if that's what you're thinking. He'd never have let us go anyway, not after he found us looking over the wall. He knew then who we were, and he must have thought we were spying on him.'

'But how did he know who we were?' Flora asked, biting her lip.

I frowned. 'I don't know. But do you remember yesterday evening when we drove out of the station yard and I told you he was watching us? Well, I was right. Some time on the journey he must have found out who we were.' I sighed. 'The worst luck was choosing his carriage to get into at Paddington.'

'But that *was* my fault,' Flora wailed. 'I chose the carriage.'

'Don't be silly,' I said. 'You couldn't possibly have known. Besides we'd have missed the train if we hadn't got in then. But why should Samuel have come down here to meet Eli Fennel?' I frowned.

'Why, to settle an old score,' Flora said suddenly, kneeling up and clapping her hands together.

'Yes,' I said. 'Yes, I believe you're right. I remember now, before he left Joel Tregarth told me that it all began a long time ago.'

'But before Samuel could find Eli Fennel he was captured and taken to that cottage,' Flora went on excitedly.

I was silent, frowning and drawing in the dust with my finger. Somehow the idea of Samuel being held prisoner seemed all wrong. It wasn't like him to let himself be trapped like that. And then, who was keeping him prisoner, and why? There was something missing, something we had left out, like a long division sum where you go wrong at the beginning but can't remember what it is you've forgotten to do. And yet it seemed the only explanation. Mrs Turvey had lied to us, and Samuel's clothes had been there in that wardrobe.

'What is it?' Flora asked, watching me.

'Nothing,' I said, jumping up and going over to the window. 'We've got to escape, that's all. Eli Fennel will be gone by tomorrow. He said himself he was taking a ship to Rotterdam.' I rubbed a patch of glass clean with the sleeve of my jacket and peered through. 'Somehow we must escape so that we can get to Samuel and warn him.'

'That's all very well,' said Flora. 'You keep saying we must escape, but how?'

'Well, there are only two ways out of this room,' I said, turning round and looking at her. 'The door's no good – so it will have to be the window.'

Flora looked at me with her mouth open and her eyes growing larger than saucers, and I looked back at her. 'Go on then,' she whispered at last, 'try the latch.'

It was very stiff, as though it hadn't been used for many years, and even after I had managed to lift it, the window still wouldn't open. It seemed to be stuck to the frame. 'What I need,' I said, 'is something which will go between the window and the frame, where it's stuck. My wood knife if I had it . . .' I felt in all my pockets, but of course I had left it at home.

Flora turned round and began to look about the room. After a minute or two she gave an exclamation and bent down. 'Would this do?' she asked, looking very pleased and coming back with a broken kitchen knife.

'It might,' I said. It had no handle and the blade was

rounded, but it was a stroke of luck finding it all the same.

'Well try it then,' Flora said excitedly.

At first it didn't work. I had to go all round the whole window twice, wiggling the knife in and out, which was stiff, warm work and took some time. I was beginning to think that the window must be barred from the outside when Flora, who had been waiting impatiently beside me, leaned forward and gave the frame an almighty crack with her clenched fist. With a groan it swung open and a gust of fresh air rushed in to greet us. Flora and I looked at each other in triumph.

Through the open window we could see the great bare shoulder of brown moorland which climbed away to the right. There were jagged outcrops of rock on the horizon and, rising up from the skyline, the tall finger of the mine that Eli Fennel had called Ding Dong pointed up to the blue sky.

'Look!' Flora said, pointing straight out to where the ground fell away behind the cottage in a patchwork of rough fields. 'There's the cottage where Samuel is.'

'It's not far,' I nodded. 'Only three fields away, and that bit of moorland. I can see smoke coming from the chimney. If only we can get out of here.'

I clambered up on to the window ledge, which was wide, and peered down at the garden below us. Directly underneath the window there was a patch of untidy grass, and beyond that a few rows of cabbages where the garden ran down to a grey stone wall which fenced it off from the moorland and fields. I guessed that the drop from the window to the ground was about two and a half times my height, but in any case it was too far to jump and the trouble was that there was no sign of a rainwater pipe, or a bench or a waterbutt or anything that would have helped us.

'Let me see, let me see,' Flora said, pulling at my jacket.

'Well, don't lean too far out,' I told her. 'Someone might see.'

She scrambled up on to the window ledge and put her head half out of the window while I leaned against the wall and tried to puzzle out how we could get down to the ground below without breaking our necks. Suddenly Flora swung round and pulled me towards the window in great excitement. 'Look!' she said, pointing in the direction of the cottage where Samuel was being held prisoner. 'There are people there. Two people. Can you see them?'

'Yes,' I nodded.

'Well, who are they?' Flora asked. 'Who do you think they are?'

I could see the men quite clearly. One of them was taking logs from a wood pile near the back door of the cottage and loading them into the other man's arms. After a moment the man carrying the logs nodded and went off into the cottage, and as he went I saw that was wearing a striped woollen hat with a bobble on it. 'That's Hodge!' I said.

'And the other one?' Flora said breathlessly, squeezing in beside me.

Left alone outside the cottage the other man looked at the sky for a moment or two and then walked across the patch of grass in a leisurely way until he reached the grey stone wall at the top of the cottage garden. I knew that walk, but it wasn't until we heard the tune that he was whistling come floating faintly across the fields that we were both sure. And at that moment we heard something else too; the click of the latch on the door below.

I grabbed Flora and pulled her back whilst I swung the window closed and pulled the latch across it. We could hear footsteps coming up the stairs and if Eli Fennel found out that we'd managed to open the window, I knew we'd be done for. I pulled Flora down beside me in the middle of the floor and we sat, trying to look dejected instead of exultant over what we'd seen. The footsteps reached the top of the stairs and stopped outside the door. We could hear Eli Fennel breathing, but he didn't come in. He must have been looking at us through the keyhole, for after a minute we heard a low chuckle and a wheezing noise as though he was getting up off his knees. Then the footsteps went back downstairs.

As soon as we heard the latch click, Flora looked up at me her eyes wide and bright. 'It *was*, wasn't it? It was Samuel.'

'No one else would whistle that tune,' I said. 'That was his marmalade tune.' We called it that because Samuel was so often whistling it and shaving when we took his breakfast tray up to him.

'We could wave something out of the window,' Flora said, jumping up. 'Then he'd see us.'

'But we mustn't make a noise,' I said. 'We mustn't let Eli Fennel hear us.' I was shaking with excitement as I pushed the latch back again and opened the window, but when we looked out again Samuel had gone and the back door of the cottage was closed.

Flora buried her face in her hands and began to cry. I felt like crying myself, only it wouldn't have done any good. Far away on one of the farms a cock was crowing and the sky above the horizon was streaked with grey clouds. 'It doesn't matter,' I whispered, closing the window again and putting my arm round her. 'We'll still escape. And don't you see . . . Samuel's not a prisoner at all.'

'It was him, wasn't it?' Flora sobbed.

'Ssh!' I said. 'Of course it was. We must have made a mistake. Don't cry any more, Flora. Eli Fennel mustn't hear us now, and I've got a plan. The window's too high from the ground for us to jump, but if we could find something to make a rope of . . .' I looked round the room.

'It's no good William,' Flora gulped, wiping her eyes on her sleeve. 'I couldn't possibly climb down a rope.'

'Yes, you could,' I said, giving her a little shake. 'It would be better than staying here, wouldn't it? And specially now we know for sure that Samuel's so close.' Flora swallowed hard, and then she nodded. 'Look round then,' I said. 'See if there's anything we could use.'

'There's the bed,' she said. 'Perhaps there's something there.' Underneath the blankets we found a cotton sheet. It was dirty and old and thin looking, but it was a start.

'It won't be long enough though, even if we tear it in half,' I said. 'And the blankets are too thick. We need something else.'

'I've got two petticoats on, one flannel and one cotton,' Flora said suddenly. 'Wouldn't they do?'

'Yes,' I nodded, 'but then you'll be cold.'

'I'll still have my skirt – and my drawers,' Flora said, turning rather pink. 'Anyway, I've been too hot all day.'

'Why do girls have to wear so many clothes?' I asked.

'It wouldn't be so bad if it weren't for all the buttons,' Flora replied, puffing a bit.

While we were making our rope the time passed quickly. It was hard work, tearing the petticoats and the sheet into strips and knotting them together, making sure that the knots would hold. Once Eli Fennel came upstairs again and we only just had time to stuff everything under the blankets before he reached our door. There was the same puffing and wheezing noise as before when he knelt down to peer through the keyhole, but he didn't say anything and we pretended to be asleep until he had gone away.

'We can't escape until it's dark,' I told Flora when the door had closed again downstairs.

'Why ever not?' she asked.

'Because we wouldn't reach the cottage without being seen,' I said.

'How long will it be?' Flora asked.

'At least another two hours,' I told her. 'But we haven't finished the rope yet.'

When it was finished Flora measured it against me to see if it was long enough, and it was almost three times my height, so we guessed that it would be all right. There was a heavy hook in the ceiling, quite close to the window, and we tied the rope to it, which wasn't easy as I had to climb on to the washstand to reach it, and it wobbled a good deal and made a noise. But Eli Fennel couldn't have heard anything, because he didn't come upstairs again. Then we swung on the rope once or twice to make sure it would take our weight, and then we took it down again and hid it.

Then the worst part of the afternoon began. We knew that Eli Fennel might come in at any moment and discover what we had been doing, or he might move us to another room, and all we could do was to sit and wait until it began to get dark, and hope that he would leave us alone. We played noughts and crosses in the dust, and then I recited 'How Horatius Held the Bridge' by Lord Macaulay, which I knew all the way through. Flora didn't know any poems except one by Wordsworth about a little girl in a graveyard and I wouldn't let her say that because we were miserable enough as it was. She knew some music hall songs though, so we went on to them.

It seemed a very long time before the light in the room began to fade and the sunlight turned from gold to pink. It had been quiet downstairs for a long while but then, suddenly, the room below us was filled with strange thumpings and clatterings and we could hear the voice of Eli Fennel and a mumbling reply which must have been his old father. Flora and I looked at each other in alarm. I wondered whether Eli Fennel would bring us a candle as it was getting dark, or whether he would think that we were hungry. I stood up and tiptoed over to the window. Very gently I opened it.

The fields were grey under the failing light and the first stars twinkled and then disappeared behind the racing dark clouds, for the wind was high and cold. I pulled out the package once more and looked at it and thought about Samuel. Even if we managed to escape we still had to find our way to the other cottage without being caught or losing our way.

'Don't you think we could go now?' Flora asked, shivering as she stood beside me. 'I feel sick.'

'Yes,' I said. 'We daren't wait any longer.'

We tied the rope to the hook and Flora listened at the door while I let it out of the window. I thought that it almost reached the ground but I couldn't quite see. Flora had done her hair in a plait so that it wouldn't get in her way, and her face was white in the gloom. I knew she was dreading going down the rope.

'You go first,' I said, giving her plait a gentle tug and grinning at her. 'Got your boots on?' She nodded. 'It'll be all right,' I said. 'You go like a sailor climbing down the rigging,' and I showed her.

She nodded. Then she took a deep breath, climbed on to the window ledge and grabbed hold of the rope. She eased herself out of the window and for a moment she hung there, too terrified to move. Then I saw her begin to slither down. The pale blur of her face went lower and lower.

'Not too fast,' I whispered. Then I heard the door open behind me and heavy footsteps coming across the room. It was too late for me to escape, but Flora might still manage to cross the moor without me and find Samuel. I pulled the precious packet out and thrust it through the window. 'The packet, Flora!' I called wildly. 'Now run ... RUN!'

'William!' I heard her call back, but by then I couldn't answer because Eli Fennel's hand came over my mouth and I was borne backwards into the room and flung to the ground.

9. Flora Alone

This is me, Flora, writing this chapter. William was going to write it and I was going to tell him what to say, because as it's all about me and he wasn't there, he wouldn't have known what to say unless I'd told him. But somehow it didn't work in the way that it should have done.

I told William what happened but when he'd written it down it didn't look right and I kept on asking him to change things and in the end William threw the pencil and paper at me and went off in a fearful huff, saying that I'd better write it myself. And so I am doing it. Only I think I ought to point out that because I'm two years younger than William my grammar probably isn't as good as his is, so there may be mistakes and I hope they will be overlooked because as Samuel says, what really matters is the story. And perhaps I'd better go back to what was happening.

There are bits that William's written about me that I don't like very much. For instance he makes out that I cry a great deal, which just isn't true. And anyway, even if I did cry once, or twice, I think anyone would have done if they'd been me, and I felt much better afterwards because crying sort of cleans you out inside. Boys always think that crying is such a dreadful thing, but it isn't at all really and I suppose that the very worst thing that happened to me was having to climb down the rope we'd made, and I didn't cry at all then.

At first I didn't think that I ever would be able to

climb down it. I felt as though my hands had turned into stones and didn't belong to me any longer, and I suppose that the only thing that made me move in the end was the thought of what would happen if Eli Fennel came into the room and caught us again. Climbing out of the window and hanging there, trying to make up my mind to move my hands, was the very worst bit of all. As soon as I had moved one of them just a little way it wasn't quite so bad and all the time I could see William at the window, smiling and nodding, which made me feel much braver. I kept wanting to look down and see how far away the ground was, only I didn't dare to, and after a while I began to have this quite horrible feeling that Eli Fennel would be waiting at the bottom for me. It was like putting your feet down to the bottom of the bed on a dark, windy night and being quite certain that there's something cold and horrible waiting to catch hold of your toes.

I thought that I'd never reach the bottom, but of course, in the end I did, and when my feet touched the ground and I let go of the rope and found there was no one there after all, I was so pleased with myself that I had done it and it was over, and so excited to be free again that, for a moment, I nearly called out. I looked up and William was still there, but instead of beginning to climb down the rope himself, he suddenly shouted at me to run and something else which I didn't hear properly.

I didn't want to go without him and I couldn't think why he was making so much noise when we'd been specially careful to be quiet all the time, so I called back to warn him. Then I heard the sound of something falling on the grass and I looked down and saw that it was the package. Eli Fennel was looking through the window. Then, of course, I realized why William had shouted and I understood that now it was all up to me. Even though I didn't want to leave William, I should have to go alone. I picked up the package from the grass and started to run.

I ran to the bottom of the garden and began to climb over the wall. I was all shaky with fright and in the dark I couldn't see where to put my feet and the stones that the wall was made of were loose, so that I slithered and slipped and grazed my knees on the top of it. But somehow I managed to get over and dropped down the other side, which was luckily only a little drop, and I began to run again.

I could hear myself making a horrid kind of gasping noise as I stumbled across the first field, and I kept looking back over my shoulder because all the time I was quite sure that Eli Fennel would be lumbering after me. I tripped on stones and tussocks of grass and several times I fell over, but I scrambled up again and went on. I ran until I simply didn't have any more breath left, and when I had to stop I looked back because I was still sure that I was being followed, but all I could see was the row of cottages dark against the sky. I couldn't see anything moving.

My sides were aching and my face felt stiff from the coldness of the wind and the way I'd been gasping, but I still had the packet clutched in my hand and all I could think of was if I just went on running then I'd come to the cottage and see Samuel. I could see a light as I climbed over the second wall, and I thought it came from the cottage where he was, only it seemed a great way off and I knew there were at least two more fields to cross.

I had never been out at night in the country before and I don't suppose that it would have seemed so bad if William had been with me. It was being quite alone that made it so especially frightening. The sky seemed to be enormous. One moment I could see stars, and then they had all disappeared because of the huge black clouds that sailed across them. What I hated most were the noises. All round me I could hear strange rustlings and scutterings. They must have been animals in the bushes at the edge of the field I suppose. Once an owl shrieked and I nearly jumped out of my skin. Even the bushes seemed like people crouching, waiting for me to come close so that they could jump out at me from the end of the field. Then I heard what sounded like someone panting up behind me, which made me look round in terror but it was only the wind.

For quite a long while I couldn't see the light from the cottage, so I thought that I had got lost and gone the wrong way. Then I came to another wall and, as I clambered up it, all at once I could see the cottage much closer with the shape of the chimney pots against the sky and it was only one field away. I slithered down the wall, grazing my legs and hands dreadfully in my hurry and, as I landed in the grass on the other side of the wall, the very worst thing of all happened.

From somewhere just behind the darkness of the bushes on my left, I heard the sound of very heavy breathing and for a while I was too frightened even to pick myself up and run. The breathing went on and on and it seemed to be coming closer. I could hear footsteps as well; very heavy footsteps coming slowly towards me. Of course I thought it was Eli Fennel coming after me, and just waiting to catch hold of me as soon as I picked myself up and began to run and I lay there, crouched on the wet grass and not daring to move with my heart beating so hard that it seemed to shake my whole body.

I probably would have stayed there for ever if the

thing hadn't come out from behind the bush. It wasn't a person at all. All that I could make out in the darkness was that it was an enormous black beast, and it was snorting and blowing, and it must have seen me moving, or smelt me, because it lowered its head and began to move towards me. I leapt up then and started to run again, and as I ran down the field I could hear the thing trotting after me. It seemed to be getting nearer and nearer, too, and by the time that I reached the last wall before the cottage and flung myself at it, I could hear the beast breathing close behind me. Somehow I managed to climb up to the top of the wall, but then I slithered and tripped on the loose stones so that at last I fell headlong into the garden and lay there, dazed and bewildered.

I heard the back door open and I tried to struggle up. Then I felt hands grabbing me and lifting me to my feet. I must have collapsed again on to the ground, for someone picked me up and carried me towards the door. 'You just come in here to the light,' said the voice that was quite distinctly Samuel's. 'I want to take a look at you, whoever you are.'

'Samuel,' I whispered, and clung to him.

'Flora? Flora! What the . . . ? My dear child. Are you all right? Are you hurt?'

'Samuel,' I said crossly, looking up at him, 'why are you wearing that ridiculous red beard and those whiskers?'

'Imperious as ever,' said Samuel, smiling at me through the whiskers. 'I grew them during the night. Now tell me what you're doing here.'

'I've come to warn you,' I said. 'We thought you were a prisoner at first, until we saw you. And then I escaped and ran all the way over the fields and I was chased by a black beast,' and I began to cry. Well, I did cry a bit then, but only because I was so pleased to see Samuel.

He carried me over to the fire and sat me on his knee and gave me a handkerchief. 'Flora,' he said gently, 'where's William?'

'Eli Fennel's still got him in the cottage,' I said.

'But that can't be, Flora,' Samuel said, looking very puzzled. 'Eli Fennel doesn't arrive in Penzance until tomorrow morning.'

'No!' I cried, shaking my head. 'No, no. He's here now. We were on the train with him yesterday.'

'You came down to Cornwall yesterday?' Samuel interrupted.

'Yes,' I said. 'You see Joel Tregarth came with the packet, just after you'd gone, and he said it was very important indeed that you should get it by last night. So we said we'd bring it to you. It was my idea.' I swallowed hard so I wouldn't begin crying again and went on. 'But when we arrived at the house you weren't there and nor was our aunt, only that horrid Mrs Turvey, and she said you'd gone and you weren't coming back, and this morning she tried to send us back to London again. Only we overheard her talking to the pedlar, Hodge, and we thought they'd taken you prisoner. They were talking about rope, you see, and we'd found all your clothes, so we knew Mrs Turvey was lying to us.'

'That woman,' said Samuel shortly, 'ought to be shot. Go on Flora.'

'That was when we ran away,' I went on, 'and we followed Hodge. It would have been all right, only then Eli Fennel found us looking over the wall just up there, and he took us back to his cottage and locked us up, so we couldn't come and rescue you. But we would have done.'

'Of course you would have done,' said Samuel, gently wiping some of the blood and mud off my hand where I had grazed it. 'But tell me, Flora, this packet that you mentioned. Have you got it now?'

'Yes,' I said proudly, pulling the oilskin packet out of my skirt pocket. 'Here!' Samuel took it from me and began to undo it at once.

'Do you hear this, Gus?' he said.

'It doesn't make sense,' said a low voice from behind me.

'On the contrary,' Samuel answered, taking some sheets of paper from inside the oilskin and looking at them. 'I think I'm beginning to understand what's happened. Your confounded Turvey has nearly ruined everything with her stupid interference. Flora,' he went on, looking up at me from the papers and smiling, 'turn round and meet your aunt. Gus, this is Flora. When her hair's brushed and she's not crying you'd be surprised how pretty she is. She's also the bravest girl in the world, I should say.'

He slid me neatly off his knee but kept his arm round me as I looked up at the figure who came forward out of the shadow behind his chair. It was easy to see that she was Samuel's sister, because she looked so like him. Her dark hair was piled on top of her head, and she wore a deep blue skirt that made a swishing noise on the ground as she moved. Her dark eyes twinkled just like Samuel's when she smiled at me, and I suddenly felt shy as I looked down at my muddy, crumpled skirt and my dusty boots that were all unlaced.

'Why do you call her Gus? It's a man's name,' I asked, leaning against Samuel.

'Wouldn't you be glad to be called Gus if you'd been christened Augusta?' Samuel asked, looking up for a moment from the papers.

'You call me Gus too,' my aunt said. 'All my real friends do.'

'It's just as I thought,' Samuel exclaimed, jumping up and waving the papers about as he paced up and down the room. 'The rogue has outwitted me again Gus.'

'Oh, Samuel,' she said softly. 'To have come so close, and now to have everything ruined.'

'We may save it yet,' Samuel said, 'but we must work quickly now I'm afraid. At the moment my first concern is for William. Eli intends to leave in the morning.'

'He won't take William with him, will he?' I gasped.

'I don't think so,' Samuel said, 'though I wouldn't put even that past him.'

'Quick,' I said, 'quick. We must go and rescue him. We'll go at once.'

'I am going,' Samuel said, taking my hand, 'just as quickly as I can. But first you must answer some questions for me Flora.'

'But I must come too,' I said.

Samuel shook his head. 'No,' he said. I looked at him. He didn't often say no, but when he did he usually meant it, and in spite of the peculiar red beard and whiskers which made him look so unlike his usual self, I could see by his eyes that he wouldn't change his mind.

'You'll never find the way,' I protested all the same. 'I know where it is you see, the cottage . . .'

'Yes,' Samuel said. 'It's old Mr Fennel's cottage. You see, I do know. You are cold and tired Flora and I want you to stay here with Gus. You've been a very good and brave girl,' he went on, speaking earnestly and looking at me in a very loving way, 'and I am proud of you. When all this is over you shall have those glacé kid boots with the buttons that you have been wanting, and more besides I daresay, but for the moment you must do just as I tell you and for the present I want you to stay here.'

'All right Samuel,' I said meekly. 'If you say that I must.'

'Good girl,' he said, as though he had expected me to make more of a fuss. 'Now tell me, which room did Eli Fennel lock you in?'

'Upstairs,' I said. 'At the back. We made a rope out of a sheet and petticoats – my petticoats.' I wasn't sure whether Samuel would be pleased about that, but he gave a little shrug and a smile so I saw that he didn't mind at all. 'I went down first,' I went on, 'but Eli Fennel came into the room just as William was going to come down and he caught him. William threw the packet to me and told me to run, and I did.'

Samuel patted my hand. 'Only one more thing,' he said. 'Was there anyone else there?'

'Just his father,' I said.

'Good!' Samuel steered me to a chair by the fire and pushed me gently into it. Then he beckoned Gus over to the door. They talked in low voices. 'I'm afraid Eli will use him as a hostage if we don't get him back,' Samuel said. 'Indeed it may be already too late.' I wasn't sure what a hostage was, but I didn't like the sound of it very much.

'Take Hodge with you,' Gus said. 'He's out in the front with the pony. And please, Samuel, be careful.'

Samuel nodded. 'Flora,' he said, 'you must stay here with Gus. No more running away. I shall be back soon, and then we'd better have a long talk.'

'Won't you please change your mind and take me,' I begged, suddenly wanting to be with him. Samuel shook his head. 'Well at least you can tell me why you're wearing that stupid red beard,' I said, joking in a rather cross way to stop myself from crying again.

Samuel laughed. 'I'll tell you tomorrow,' he said. 'I promise. And for now will it content you if I say that it all concerns Mr Lucifer?' He blew me a kiss, held Gus's hand for a moment and before I could ask any more questions he was gone, closing the door behind him.

Left alone together for the first time, Gus and I looked at each other. 'I suppose Hodge is on our side?' I asked.

Gus nodded. 'He's our chief spy. And that's the only question I'm going to answer, because Samuel will tell you everything later. Besides,' she put her head on one side a little and looked at me, 'I think it's time we tidied you up a bit. You look a real ragamuffin at present.'

When she had done my hair and I had washed my face and hands and tucked in my blouse and taken off my stockings which were all torn and stained with mud because I had gone without my boots, I did feel much better. I curled up in a chair beside the fire and Gus brought me a slice of ham and two pieces of cake.

'It's all rather a picnic for the moment,' she said, 'but I daresay we shall do better later on.' Then she kicked the logs into a blaze and sat down in the chair opposite me while I ate. For the first time since we left Kennington I felt warm and happy and safe.

I must have closed my eyes quite soon afterwards, because suddenly everything that had happened that day and the day before seemed to be rushing away from me down a long dark tunnel: first the train, and Gus's smile, then the rope we had made and Samuel's red beard; Eli Fennel laughing as he dug his fork into the rabbit stew and Mrs Turvey looking angry and her red cheeks wobbling with fury; and the Chinese cabinet in Gus's drawing-room. I tried to open my eyes again, because I wanted to stay awake until Samuel came back, but it wasn't any good ...

When I woke up I was being lifted up and set on a high seat. I opened my eyes and saw a thousand stars and the wind was cold on my face. 'It's all right,' Samuel said, as he tucked the rug round me, 'we're going back to Gus's house in the pony trap.'

'Where's William?' I asked.

'You'll see him in the morning,' Samuel said.

Gus climbed up in the trap beside me and put her arm round me. 'Go back to sleep,' she said. I heard the rumble of wheels and the soft clopping of the pony's hooves as we set off. 'It'll be all right in the morning. You and I are going to dress up as fish wives and meet William at the harbour ...'

Well, that was what I thought she said, but then I was half asleep.

10. The Old Shaft

I hadn't been looking forward to climbing down the rope myself, although I would never have let Flora see that I was frightened, but all the same I would willingly have changed places with her and made off across the moor rather than stay in that room with Eli Fennel.

He was horribly angry that Flora had escaped, but he didn't try to go after her as I was afraid he would. He just stared at me, literally grinding his teeth together and clenching and unclenching his hands as though he would like to throttle me. I was too petrified even to move from where he had hurled me, and all that I could think about was what he would do next. He looked so furious that I thought he might beat me – or worse. Then, all at once, an idea seemed to come to him and his mood changed. He smiled, and came towards me, chuckling harshly.

'Very good, very good Master Rolandson,' he said, pulling me to my feet and bundling me roughly towards the door. 'But first of all we'll clip your wings eh? Shackle you with a ball and chain, eh? We can't have you trying any more tricks, not when everything is drawing to an end – so . . .'

By now we had reached the kitchen. Eli Fennel pushed me on to one of the chairs and, seizing a coil of rope from the table, he began to truss me up like a chicken ready for the oven. The rope hurt my wrists and I felt as though I could barely breathe; but the worst thing to bear was the gloating look of satisfaction on his face.

'They'll come for me you know,' I said, hoping that I sounded braver than I felt. 'You can't keep me a prisoner here. Flora will fetch help – the police I expect.'

Eli chuckled. 'I fancy they'll come for you all right,' he agreed. 'If little Flora manages to get across Woon Gumpus Common – because that's what it's called, that bit of moorland out there. It's not a pleasant place at night. Besides the marsh, and the rabbit holes that she could put her foot down and trip in, there are things moving about at night out there that are older than the hills – and a great deal nastier.' He put his face close to mine and smiled. 'I hope your little sister's not frightened of ghosts,' he said, 'because if she is she could end up in the cold light of dawn wandering round with her five wits gone . . .' He waved his hand at the ceiling, still looking at me.

I swallowed. 'It's no use trying to frighten me,' I said. 'I know that Flora will fetch help and she's not in the least scared of ghosts.'

'Maybe she will then,' Eli said softly. 'But by the time she comes back here with help, you and I will be gone.' He paused for a moment and then went on. 'I've got work to do tonight, and you're coming with me, Billy boy. So if you're wise you'll sit quiet and rest while you have the chance.' He chuckled. 'You've got a busy night in front of you. You're going to be a great help to me.'

'I shan't help you,' I muttered.

'Well, then, I say you will,' Eli Fennel answered, 'for if you don't it'll be the worse for you.'

'No matter what you do to me I won't help,' I said.

He ignored me and went on speaking. 'You're useful to me, Billy boy,' he said, picking up a canvas bag from the floor and putting it on the table. 'The fact is, you're more than useful – you're invaluable.' He leaned on the table and spoke softly. 'You're my safe conduct until I go aboard that ship tomorrow morning – the one that's bound for Rotterdam as I told you. No one's going to harm a hair of my head, least of all Samuel Rolandson, who'd dearly love to see me . . .' He paused and drew his finger across his throat. 'As I said, no one's going to harm a hair of my head so long as you're in front of me and this is against your back.' He moved his hand slowly across the table until it came to rest beside a heavy pistol. His dark eyes were watching my face and he tapped the pistol lazily once or twice and then gave a smile of satisfaction when he saw me start. 'So you be a good boy,' he went on, 'and you and I will work together tonight as harmoniously as your pa and I did when we were out in Kimberley together and the best of pals.'

I hated him then for using me against Samuel, and I was full of helpless fury. I remembered the Winter Mixture sweet that he had given to Flora on the train, and I hoped that one day I might have the chance to pay him back for what he was doing. But for the moment I would have to do as he said.

'That's better Billy boy,' he smiled. 'I knew you'd be more obedient and reasonable in the end.' He began to make preparations to leave the cottage and I sat silent, watching him. I wondered where Flora was now, and whether she had found her way to the cottage and was with Samuel, or whether she had got lost or worse.

Then, quite suddenly, it came to me. The bit that had been missing when I'd tried to work things out earlier, the bit of the long division sum. I stared hard at the rope round my wrists and inside my mind everything seemed to turn upside down – for Eli Fennel had thought we were watching him when we were looking over the wall! That was why he had crept up behind us, hoping to give us a nasty fright. That was why he had said, later on, that he was surprised at Samuel using us to spy on him. That meant that he didn't know that Samuel was close, that he was in that cottage, just three fields away. Eli Fennel didn't know where Samuel was at all! He thought that Flora would have to run miles and miles, to the nearest police station to fetch help, but if he knew how close Samuel was to us, he wouldn't be so smug.

I felt a warm glow begin to grow inside me, and for a moment I wondered whether I was going to cry because it was so wonderful to think that any moment now, Samuel would be here to rescue me. Flora would be sure to reach the cottage. It wasn't far, and she knew where it was. All she had to do was to get there, and explain to Samuel and tell him where I was. He would come. He would be here quite soon.

I thought I had been so careful and that I wasn't giving myself away. I didn't smile, or turn round to look at the door. I just went on staring at the rope round my wrists and trying not to show that I was listening for the sound of footsteps outside. But I wasn't careful enough. Suddenly the room was very quiet. The silence was unnatural.

I looked up and Eli Fennel was watching me. He was standing stock still on the other side of the table and his black eyes seemed to bore into my mind. 'You're expecting someone, aren't you Billy boy?' he said. I shook my head, but it was no good. He knew. 'Yes you are,' he said, narrowing his eyes. 'Samuel Rolandson must be closer than I'd taken account of. I never thought of that.' He smiled, and then went to the door and listened. There was no sound. 'Well,' he said, 'I'll not stay here to be caught like a rat in a trap.

My old father's upstairs in bed and fast asleep by now, I daresay. This very minute will be as good a time as any to go.'

He hitched the canvas bag over his shoulder, and then he came over and began to untie me. I thought for one moment that he was going to let me go. Instead, he left one end of the rope knotted around my waist, while the other he tied to his own belt. Then, with a final look around the dark cottage, he opened the door and without waiting to blow out the candle on the kitchen table, he pushed me outside.

He had not been a moment too soon, for we were only just outside the front gate when he clapped a hand over my mouth and pulled me down behind the shelter of the wall. Coming around the side of the cottage there were two figures. Eli held his hand tightly over my mouth and his other arm was round me in an iron grip so that I could neither move nor cry out.

We watched as the two figures disappeared under the shadow of the porch and then Eli pulled me roughly to my feet and pushed me before him along the lane. 'One squeak,' he whispered in my ear, 'and it'll be the last you make.'

I felt the hard lump of the pistol against my back so that I dared not even turn round and look back. As I stumbled on, farther and farther away from my rescuers, hot angry tears sprang into my eyes and blurred the brightness of the stars. Eli took to the open moor almost at once, and we left the path behind us.

The going was rough, and he cursed as he tripped over the stones which lay, half hidden, under the heather. I staggered along beside him, doing my best to keep up. Sometimes the moon came out from behind a cloud and then I could see his face. He no longer smiled. Instead he had a grim, desperate look that made me fearful when I looked at him, and he glanced often over his shoulder.

The moon came and went, but the wind never stopped. It was cold and strong, and it blew in gusts, shrieking and moaning, right into our faces as though wanting to turn us back. Before long my ears were aching with cold, and my jacket, which had seemed so hot and thick that morning, flapped round me. I shivered with cold and my footsteps began to drag. I thought longingly of blazing fires and my own warm bed at home.

'Are you going to walk faster, Billy boy, or do I have to drag you along?' Eli Fennel growled at last, turning round and glaring at me. By now I had dropped back and there was the length of the rope between us.

'I can't keep up,' I stammered. 'I'm so cold. Couldn't we have a rest?'

Eli shook his head, and came back and took me by the shoulder. 'See!' he said, pointing towards the horizon where the tall finger of the deserted tin mine could be seen against the sky. 'That's where we're going. To Ding Dong, the mine I told you about this morning. There's a shaft there . . .' He broke off and chuckled. 'Well, you'll see soon enough when we get there, Billy boy.' He slung the canvas bag off his back and felt inside it. 'Here,' he said. 'Put this on. It'll help keep this cursed wind off you. And you can have the muffler as well.'

Gratefully I struggled into the ragged leather waist-coat which he handed me. It was far too large, but the muffler, being enormously long, I wound that round my head and neck, crossed it over my chest and tied it at the back. The muffler smelled evil, but it was made of silk and wonderfully warm.

Eli Fennel stared at me in the moonlight and for a

moment his face looked almost gentle. 'You're an odd enough sight now,' he said, 'but you'll need to keep warm for what lies ahead. How old are you Billy boy?'

'Twelve, sir,' I muttered.

'Then it must be twelve years since I visited Ding Dong. Twelve years eh? Long enough you'd think to throw the hounds off the scent. Long enough to shake free of the past.' His voice had become harsh again. 'But not long enough for Samuel Rolandson, curse him,' he growled, and he gave a sudden, sharp jerk to the rope which bound us together. 'Now keep up, boy, and don't lag behind.'

We went on for some time after that in silence and gradually the pointing finger of the mine grew clearer. I suppose that we had been walking for about an hour when we left the moorland and turned into a lane. The way was easier there, and for the time being Ding Dong was lost from our view behind the steep banks which rose up on each side of us. The wind could not reach us down there, and in the sudden silence I heard the sound of our feet on the rutted track and Eli Fennel's heavy breathing just ahead of me.

'We will be there soon, boy,' he said over his shoulder.

'What will happen when we arrive?' I asked, for the dread of what might be ahead was stealing all my courage.

'You'll see soon enough,' was Eli's only reply.

After dipping down for a little way the lane began to rise again and ran out on to the open moorland once more. Just ahead of us, huge and menacing against the moonlit sky, was the tall chimney of the mine. Eli Fennel stopped and looked around in silence for some minutes. He was breathing hard and he pulled me on towards a grassy bank which ran up to the very walls of the mine. There he began to nod and mutter under his breath. I watched, fascinated, but afraid that he had gone mad. I realized with relief, after a minute or two, that he was only working something out.

At last, satisfied with his calculations, he grabbed me by the wrists and put his face close to mine. 'Now you're to follow me, and keep hard by, Billy boy, for if you don't you may wish you had. There are shafts around here that are deeper than the knowledge of man. Do you know what a shaft is?' he asked. I shook my head and took a step backwards.

He laughed. 'A shaft is a hole that goes down, into the ground, deep, deep into the black bowels of the earth, Billy boy. That's where the tin is you see. Down in the earth. That's where the miners have to go to fetch it up. And when they can't find any more in one hole, after maybe twenty years or so, why then they dig another hole. But they don't bother to fill them in when the workings are finished, so you and I will have to walk carefully.'

'How many are there?' I whispered.

'Quite a few around here,' Eli said. 'I told you this mine had been worked since before the time of Jesus Christ, didn't I?' He smiled slowly. 'But don't worry, because I know where they all are, and where the one is that we've got to find. Quite a spot to hide my treasure, don't you think so, Billy boy?'

'What treasure?' I asked, staring at him.

'You know what treasure,' he snarled. 'Come on now, follow me. And no false steps, mind.'

I felt cold and sick as I followed Eli. All around us I could see the shapes of bramble and gorse bushes and I knew that hidden there, beneath the tangled undergrowth, there were shafts. Slowly and as surely as a cat, Eli picked his way along the tiny paths which ran through the bushes, until at last he gave a chuckle and nodded. Just ahead I saw a low hedge of brambles curving round in a circle in the moonlight.

'Here we are then,' he muttered. 'Nice and safe.' He took a sickle from his bag and hacked a way through the brambles and gorse, moving forward very carefully as he did so. Then he turned round and came back towards me.

'Thirsty?' he asked. He took a bottle of cold tea out of his bag and a piece of bread and cheese. 'Go on,' he said, seeing me hesitate, although I was hungry and thirsty. 'It's not poisoned you know.' He watched me eat and drink, nodding with satisfaction, and then beckoned me towards the edge of the shaft. I shrank back and he laughed at me. 'I'm not going to push you in Billy boy,' he said. 'I told you before, only I think you must have forgotten, you're invaluable to me.'

When I was beside him, he pulled a stone out of the ground and, leaning over, he tossed it into the blackness below. I heard the hollow sound as it bounced against the walls of the shaft. The sound became fainter, but it did not stop for a long time.

'Four . . . five . . . six . . .' Eli counted. After that we could hear it no longer. 'But it's still going,' he whispered in my ear. 'I'd say that no one would think of looking here. I'd say that my treasure will still be hidden, safe and sound in this shaft, even after twelve years, wouldn't you, Billy boy?' I didn't answer. 'You don't know, do you? Or you're not saying. Whichever it is we shall soon see. There's just one trouble though, Billy. I'm not as agile as I used to be – not so nimble.' He put his hand on my shoulder. 'So you'll have to go down there and fetch it up for me.'

'No!' I whispered. I felt my stomach turn over and my hands were clammy with sweat. 'No. I can't and I won't.'

'Yes!' Eli whispered. And then he took hold of me and shook me so that I could feel my teeth rattling. 'I'm a desperate man,' he said, still quietly. 'I've travelled thousands of miles to collect my treasure and I'll not be baulked now. So you'd best do as I tell you if you want to see the light of day again.'

'But I'll fall,' I said.

Eli shook his head. 'Have no fear of that. You do as I say and I promise you, Billy boy, you'll come to no harm. I'll bring you up again safe and sound and I'll make certain you don't fall. Don't forget that I need you until I get on to that ship in the morning. The only way you can come to harm is by refusing to do what I say. But you won't do that, will you now? I know you won't.' He laughed at me and clapped me on the shoulder, and then he took a deep breath and said, 'Samuel thought to use you to baulk me. But I've out-witted him, because now you're my invaluable little slave.'

He hammered an iron stake into the soft ground beside the shaft and then, undoing the end of the rope that was around his waist, he tied it to the stake. 'Now when you gets in there,' he said, 'you start to count the rows of bricks from the top of the shaft, calling out as you go down. I'll pay out the rope nice and slow and it'll be tied tight around your waist, so you've no need to be fearful. One hand for the rope and one to count the bricks. Do you see?' I nodded. My heart was thumping wildly. 'When you get down to the twentieth row I'll tell you what to do. Ready now?'

Eli tightened the rope around my waist and put his hand on my shoulder almost kindly. 'The sooner it's begun the sooner it'll be over,' he said. In spite of my own fear I noticed that his voice was shaking.

Fumbling with fright, I slithered myself backwards over the lip of the shaft, holding the rope with both hands. I could feel the deathly cold air swirling upwards from the unknown depths and wrapping itself around my legs and, for a moment, although I was tied, I dared not let go of the rope even with one hand. I thought of myself suspended by only a rope above that abyss, and I closed my eyes. 'Please,' I gasped. 'I can't do it.'

'Go on, boy,' Eli said hoarsely and without pity. 'Start counting.' He looked at me over the edge of the shaft, his eyes black and his lips twitching and I knew that if I refused his fury would be uncontrollable. I slithered my hand from the rope, gritting my teeth together and feeling for the first row of bricks.

'One!' I called. 'Two. Three.' Each time I called out, Eli lowered me a little farther. It seemed to go on for ever and the crawling blackness below came up to meet me and surrounded me absolutely. I was in another world. Far above I could see the brightness of the stars. At last I reached the twentieth row and called it out, but from above there was silence. 'Where are you?' I shrieked in sudden terror.

'Easy boy,' Eli answered, peering at me down the shaft. 'Easy now. Feel along the row and you'll find there's a brick loose.'

I moved my hand along slowly, wiggling the damp, cold bricks with the edges of my fingers. 'No,' I called. 'They're all tight. There isn't one loose.'

'Try the other direction, Billy boy. And remember, it's been twelve years. There may be moss and earth around it. Take it easy now.'

I began again. One, two, three, four. No good. Five,

six. Still no good. I had gone as far as my arm would stretch when I felt it. A small movement. I wiggled a bit more. 'I've found it,' I called out, excited in spite of myself. I pulled, and the brick fell from its place and went crashing down into the blackness below. The endless bang . . . bang . . . bang made me feel giddy. I leaned my head against the side of the shaft, holding the rope with both hands again.

'You all right, Billy boy?' Eli called.

'Yes,' I answered.

'Good lad. Now take care how you do this. Put your hand inside and you'll feel a space. A largish space. All right?'

'Yes,' I answered, wriggling one hand into the hole.

'At the back there's a canvas bag. Get a good grip on it lad. Mind you don't let that fall and follow the brick – or I'll not answer for the consequences. Pull it out now and I'll haul you up again. Call when you're ready.'

I could hear that his voice was shaking with impatience and excitement now, but it wasn't easy to squeeze the bag through the gap, and my hands were shaking. Slowly I edged it towards me, holding tight to it, for my life depended upon it, and I was sick with terror at the thought of what would happen if I let it fall.

'Haul me up!' I called at last, clutching the bag against my chest and, with wonderful relief, I felt myself beginning to rise slowly – so slowly – but each moment drew me closer to the top.

Eli barely let me scramble over the edge of the shaft before he seized the bag from my arms and with shaking hands started to slit it open with his knife. I rolled away and lay for a moment, breathing the clean, cold air and blinking at the stars.

The moon had ridden out from behind a cloud when I looked at Eli again, and I could see that he had forgotten me. There, lying on the rags in which it had been hidden for so long, was a stone as big as an egg, which flashed and shone with a fiery light.

'Is it a diamond?' I whispered, moving closer as though drawn towards it.

Eli held me back with his arm and would not let me touch it. 'It's a diamond all right,' he said softly. 'About the largest diamond that ever came off the Blue Ground at Kimberley.'

11. Mr Lucifer

After a while the moon went behind a cloud and Eli Fennel seemed to rouse himself as though from a dream. He began to wrap the diamond up again in its cloths, and as he did so he crowed and chuckled and shook his head from side to side with pleasure. I think he had forgotten that I was there, for he paid no attention to me and suddenly I saw that my chance to escape had come at last. We were no longer lashed together because Eli had tied his end of the rope to the iron stake before he sent me down the shaft. Slowly and quietly, keeping my eyes on him all the time, I began to edge away.

Eli was too cunning for me. 'You'll understand that I've waited a longish time for that jewel, Billy boy,' he said suddenly, without turning round or raising his voice. 'I'd not care for anything to go wrong now; so be a good lad and stay where you are, will you, and you and I will finish up the best of pals tomorrow morning.' I stopped, and it was just as well that I did, for when he turned round I saw that he was holding the pistol in his hand.

He smiled at me. 'I'd like to think that we'll part good friends,' he said, 'even though we go our separate ways, for you've done me a great service tonight, Billy boy. I shall think of that when I'm on my way to my darling little farm in South America – and you're back in Samuel's loving arms.'

I looked away from him and up at the stars. I wouldn't have had the strength to run anywhere in any case, for my teeth were chattering with cold and fright, and I felt weak and empty inside now that it was all over. But most of all, I think, I was filled with a kind of despair, because at last I understood why Samuel had come to Cornwall and I saw that all his plans were overthrown.

'Cold, Billy boy?' Eli asked, peering at me. 'Well – I daresay you are. Mine shafts are damp, cold things as nobody knows better than me, for I've spent a lifetime down them. But we don't need to wait here any longer now that our work's done. We'll find a sheltered spot and build a fire.' He picked up his canvas bag and slung it over his shoulder. Then, motioning me to follow he led the way back towards the lane.

'Not frightened of ghosts are you, boy?' he asked, as we turned up a track which led out again on to the open moor. 'Because the place we're going to is haunted, so they say.' I did not answer, thinking that he was only trying to frighten me, and wishing that he would leave me alone. I thought that I was too tired to be frightened of anything more, but I must admit that I started and shrank back when I saw the shape which loomed up in front of us.

'Come on boy, it don't bite,' Eli chuckled, taking my arm and urging me towards it. 'And haunted or not, it'll shelter us from this accursed wind.'

The thing looked like some gigantic, nightmare animal, crouching motionless on the moorland and waiting for us to draw close enough so that it could spring, but as we came near to it, I hated myself for having shown that I was frightened, for it was only a group of enormous stones. They were arranged like a giant milking stool, and the top one was as tall as Eli Fennel himself.

'They do say our ancestors used to be buried under

here,' Eli said, 'and that would be why it's so ghostly, wouldn't you say so Billy boy?' He still hoped to scare me, but now I only smiled, for the stones no longer frightened me and I felt that the place was friendly. I was glad that we were going to stay there.

I had to help Eli to gather furze and heather for our fire. He cut the roots with his knife and I carried the bundle. When we had as much as I could carry we went back to the stones, and Eli built a fire where there was no wind and it was sheltered.

It was the best fire I ever saw in my life, even though it was he who built it, and I don't think I ever thought anything so beautiful as the brightness and warmth of the flames as they began to crackle into life. Eli warmed up a can of tea and he gave me a piece of bread to dip in it. He drank some of the tea, but left most of it me and drank instead from a hip flask which he pulled out of his pocket.

He was pleased with himself, now that he had got the diamond back again, and as he drank he began to chuckle and talk as though we were old friends. He told me about the first time he went down the mines, back over the hill at Boscaswell, and he didn't seem to notice that I didn't answer him. My toes were warm, and my face was warm and I was so sleepy that I felt as though I was in a dream. I even felt warm inside after the tea and bread and I would have liked to curl up beside the fire and go fast asleep. I think that I did drowse off for a little while, but then Eli shook me and told me to put more furze on the fire.

'If I can't sleep,' he said, 'you shan't either. Tomorrow, when I'm safely gone, you can sleep, Billy boy. But not now. I can't have you escaping, can I, eh? Besides, I'm going to tell you the whole story of the diamond. You'd like that, wouldn't you? Night time round the fire – that's the time for telling stories.' He laughed and dug me in the ribs. 'There won't be any Zulus tonight, I promise you that. And no one to rescue you either. Just you and me and the diamond, eh lad?'

'I don't want to hear the story,' I said sullenly.

'But you'll have to listen just the same,' he chuckled gleefully. 'Oh I daresay that Samuel told you a good deal before he set you both to spy on me – but now you can hear my side of it.' He looked at me and shook his head solemnly. 'I'm afraid you didn't make a very good spy, Billy boy. You'd best stick to mining, I'd say. Why – I knew who you both were before the train reached Bristol.'

'How did you know it was us?' I asked.

Eli laughed and took another drink from his flask. 'If you want to travel incognito – and that's what it's called among spies, Billy boy, when they don't wish to be recognized – ' he lowered his voice and went on confidentially, leaning close to me, 'why, then you mustn't print your name on your luggage, must you?'

So that was it! I looked at the fire and saw in my mind's eye, as clearly as though it were there in front of me, the label that Nellie had written, sitting at the kitchen table at home. 'Rolandson. Passenger to Penzance.' I smiled.

'Mind you,' Eli went on, 'Miss Flora took me by surprise at first. But then I reckoned that it was like Samuel to collect a bunch of brats around him, soft-hearted fool that he is. Any more of you at home, Billy?' I didn't answer, but I wished I could have found the courage to hit him.

There was silence for a little while and when I looked up I found to my surprise that Eli was looking at me with an oddly gentle expression. 'You,' he said, jabbing a stubby finger at me, 'now you reminded me of someone. A woman. I saw the likeness at once.' He sighed, and his expression changed again. He took another drink. 'But that's a long time ago,' he said harshly, 'and what's more important to us, here and now, is that you and Miss Flora must have had quite a nasty surprise when you turned round and found me standing behind you.'

He threw another bit of furze on the fire. 'You were watching the wrong cottage, weren't you? Samuel always was a fool,' he laughed. 'Just to think that a pair of brats would be any use as spies. Only Samuel would think of that.' He laughed again. 'He's too soft you see, Billy boy, and begging your pardon, for I'm sure you're fond enough of him. But you see it doesn't do to think too well of people.

'Why, when we were out in Kimberley, Samuel thought he knew me pretty well and he trusted me too. Loved me like a brother he said, and all because I saved his life once in a drinking house brawl. Bah! I'd have done the same for anyone,' Eli said scornfully. 'But he didn't know that, the fool!' He spat into the fire. 'Mind you I was glad enough of his company, but I was there for the diamonds. You can't live on friendship. I'd been down the mines for fifteen years when I got out to Africa, and never a penny to show for it.'

He grabbed my arm suddenly and pushed his face close to mine. 'Have you any idea what it's like to go down into the bowels of the earth every day, Billy boy? To work in the dark and cold, far from the sunlight and fresh air, where there's nothing but danger to keep you company and it takes you half an hour to reach the surface again when your day's work is done? You can be buried alive, down in a mine, and suffocate to death before help comes to you. Many's the time I've worked till I ached all over, but somehow you've got to go on to the end of your shift, no matter how you ache. And at the end of it all, when you come to the top, you've no more than a few shillings to show for it all, and a cottage as damp and rotten and ugly as the one you saw today. You didn't think much of that, did you, boy? Oh yes, I saw your face when you came through the door, and the way you looked at the mud floor and the few sticks of furniture. Well I didn't think a deal of it either. I wanted to be rich and that's why I went to Kimberley – and nothing wrong with that is there? The Cornish miners are the best in the world, you know.'

I winced. 'Please sir,' I muttered. 'My arm . . .'

'Only trouble was, though,' he said, letting go at last, 'I never had any luck. All around me other men were finding diamonds, and big ones too. They'd make a find and then sell their claim to the land and go home, rich for life. The man in the next valley found one the size of a walnut, but not me. Each day I'd say to myself, "This is the day, Eli". And each day ended and I'd found nothing. Nothing . . .'

He paused and gazed deep into the fire. 'One day,' he went on, 'I got back to the camp and found Samuel packing. When I asked him why, he said that there was a party leaving for the coast in the morning, and he didn't reckon that Kimberley would have much more to offer him after what he'd just found. I could see that he was excited, and being Samuel he couldn't keep it to himself for long. He put his arm round me and he pulled the stone out and showed it to me, close, mind you, so that no one else could see. Well at first I couldn't believe it, Billy boy. I'd seen stones the size of walnuts; one as big as a bantam's egg. But this one . . . It lay in Samuel's hand, and it flashed and sparkled as though it was enchanted. You see it wasn't just that it was big. It was more than that – the fire in it and the colour. Well, after a while he put it away again and went on packing. But he saw me looking forlorn, which I was, and lo and behold if he doesn't ask me to come to the coast as well, and when he sells the diamond he'll see me all right. More than enough for both of us, he says. The fool!'

Eli paused and clenched his hands together, gazing deep into the fire. 'I didn't want his waterish charity,' he said softly. 'I knew that I'd never find a stone like that now, for there wouldn't be another one like it. I cursed my luck that it should have been him to uncover such a beauty and not me, which by rights I thought it ought to have been. And after a little while I made up my mind to have it off him, come what might. So I said I'd go with him in the morning and thanked him for his kindness.' Eli put the flask away in his pocket and laughed. Then he shook his head, but he didn't speak for a long time.

'Go on,' I said at last, because I couldn't help myself.

'What? Oh, yes,' he said, looking at me and seeming to recollect. 'Yes. Well, off we went.' He thought for a moment. 'I was waiting my chance all the time, not knowing when it might come, but determined that I'd be there when it did. For a long time it seemed as though it would be impossible. Samuel kept the stone in a bag which he hung round his neck; he was a light sleeper, too. I had almost given up hope when the Zulus came along, just in the nick of time. All the territory between Kimberley and Durban was dangerous for the white man to cross just then, you see Billy boy, for the Zulus were growing snappish – and travelling for upwards of five hundred miles by ox cart with women and children wasn't the fastest way of going either. The Zulu would attack at night, and the plan was always the same. When you hear the feet thundering and the spears rattling, form a ring with the wagons. Everyone inside the ring, and try to fight them off – the trouble was though, the Zulus usually won, there being a great number of them.'

Eli kicked the fire which was dying down, with his boot, and then looked at me with a smile. 'Well, we went along quite peaceful for a good time, but one night we heard those thunderous feet and we knew we were for it all right. I fancied I'd have a better chance outside the ring, though,' he said slyly, 'so I slipped off before the fun began and hid myself in a tree until it was all over. When dawn came and the Zulus finally took themselves off, down I crept, safe and sound and did a little tour of inspection. It was an ugly sight, as I daresay you know. I found Samuel easily enough, and taking him for dead, which all the rest were, I bent down and cut the cord that held the bag round his neck. Imagine my surprise, Billy boy, when he groans and opens his eyes. He stared straight at me, and of course he saw at once how things were. He gave me a good, long look, but he couldn't do much more, because by then my knife was at his throat.' Eli paused. Then he frowned. 'Do you know what he said then, Billy boy?' he asked.

'No,' I answered, shaking my head.

'He said "Lucifer". That was all. Just the one word and nothing else. Now what do you think he meant by that?'

I looked into the red, glowing heart of the fire and said nothing. I couldn't have spoken, even I had wanted to, for the lump in my throat and I was thinking of how Samuel had joked about Eli Fennel's treachery and kept the secret all these years. Mr Lucifer had come home all right, but he was about to slip from Samuel's grasp once more, and I wished from the bottom of my heart that there was something that I could do.

'I don't know why he called me Lucifer,' Eli muttered. 'I've been puzzling over that for years. You might ask him when you see him, will you?' I nodded. 'Good,' he said. 'Anyway, I didn't wait to find out what he meant then. I took one of the horses and galloped off as hard as I could, leaving Samuel to the vultures – him and the squealing baby I could hear. I suppose that was you, was it Billy?'

Suddenly his expression changed again. 'I should have slit Samuel's throat and saved myself a deal of trouble,' he growled. 'As it was I haven't had a moment's peace from that day to this. Who would have thought that he'd have reached the coast? Anyway, before I knew where I was I began to hear stories of how he'd found the biggest diamond on the Blue Ground and had it stolen by his best friend. That was bad. That meant that I had to disappear, and quick. It meant that I couldn't sell the stone either, because it would be sure to be recognized. So I came back home and I hid the diamond in the safest place I knew.' He sighed. 'For twelve years I've been waiting to come and collect it. I went to Australia first, and then I went to South America, and at last I thought I'd shaken Samuel off my tail – but the fool always did stick closer than a shadow. Never mind, I've had my revenge tonight, Billy boy, and sweet it's been.' He chuckled. 'Be sure to tell him how you went down the mine shaft and brought the diamond up for me, won't you Billy boy. Don't forget now . . .' He grabbed me by the arm and pulled me round to face him and he laughed at me again.

'Let go of me,' I cried, pushing my hand against his chest. 'You're not free *yet*, Mr Fennel. Samuel's the best person I've ever known, and whatever you may think you haven't beaten him *yet*. So you needn't think you have. You're not on that ship *yet*.' I felt his grip tighten on me and he stopped laughing and raised his arm as though he would hit me. I glared back at him in the firelight, no longer caring if he did.

'If Samuel Rolandson gets in my way before that ship sails,' Eli growled at last, 'I'll blow your brains out, Billy boy.'

12. The Stone Changes Hands

I sat with my knees huddled up, watching the dying embers of the fire and at last the sky turned from black to grey and the outline of the huge stones became clearer.

The sun was rising as we made our way back towards the road which led down to the coast. I tripped and stumbled with tiredness, but I spoke not a word to Eli Fennel and he did not talk to me. Where the lane met the road a little grey donkey waited patiently in the shafts of a cart. The reins were hitched to a gatepost. Although there was no one in sight Eli must have expected that the cart would be waiting, for he motioned me to climb in and, unhitching the reins from the post, he got up beside me. In the back of the cart there were two small, tin trunks, both corded down, and a carpet bag.

Eli was uneasy and irritable now that morning had come. He did not talk at all, but remained sunk in a deep, gloomy silence, moving only to slap the reins impatiently against the donkey's back or to look over his shoulder. He looked bleary and his eyes were bloodshot. Sometimes his lips moved as though he was talking to himself. By then I was too tired for fear, but I knew that he was desperate and ready to fly into a rage should anything happen to stop him from boarding the ship. All I cared about now was that it would all soon be over; a huge wave of weariness seemed to engulf me and the brightness of the morning and the song of the birds as we rode along were dreamlike.

In a while the road dipped down and ran through a little wood, very like the one where Flora and I had hidden the day before. Eli turned the donkey's head to the hedge and jumped down.

'Give me the muffler and jacket,' he growled, and waited impatiently as I struggled out of them. Then he bound my hands and feet and throwing a cloth over me, so that no one should see if they happened to come by that I was tied up, he took the carpet bag from the cart and disappeared amongst the trees.

Below, in the valley, I could hear a stream bubbling over stones. Birds chirruped in the trees and the donkey cropped the grass off the top of the wall, lifting its head occasionally to listen to some sound. I supposed that Eli would come back some time, but I half wished that the morning might stop where it was and never go on.

Before long he returned, climbing up through the wood. He had changed once again into the smart clothes that he had worn in the train and he must have washed his face in the stream and combed his hair, for he looked clean and refreshed. He carried his bowler hat in one hand and the carpet bag in the other. Altogether he presented quite a smart appearance as he clambered up into the cart again beside me and undid the rope around my wrists. I don't suppose that anyone but me would have noticed the bulge in his pocket where the pistol lay.

'You know it's there, and I know it's there,' he said quietly, leaning close to me and peering into my face, 'but I hope I shan't have call to use it, Billy boy.' He stuffed the rope into the carpet bag and we set off again. 'Now as we goes along, we're going to see people. Lots of 'em when we get down to the harbour, I daresay. But don't you make the mistake of thinking that you can cut and run for it, because if you try it, you know what'll happen, don't you?'

'Yes, sir,' I murmured.

He nodded. 'You and I understand one another pretty well by now, I reckon,' he said. 'I've half a mind to take you with me, Billy boy. What would you think of that eh? How would you like to come to South America with me?'

'I'd rather stay in England,' I said, looking to see whether he really meant it.

'Well, well,' he chuckled, his good spirits returning a little. 'Perhaps it's just as well. You know too much for my comfort I daresay, and I couldn't keep you always at a rope's end, could I?'

'I won't forget what you've done for me, Billy boy,' he said later on. 'You're a plucky lad and though you led me a dance to begin with, you saw sense in the end. Samuel's a lucky man to have you. But if I could choose between you and the diamond, then I'd still choose the stone, I reckon.' He laughed, but this time it was a melancholy laugh, and looking round I saw that he seemed suddenly to have grown smaller, as though he had shrunk a little.

It was still early as we drove through the town and there were very few people about. The shutters were still up on most of the shops and the wheels of our little cart seemed to rumble like thunder in the narrow streets. The sun had gone in, though it was so early, and long, grey clouds were banking up in the sky. As we rounded the last corner and saw the bay below us, the wind whipped into our faces and the sea was white with waves. It looked as though Eli would have a rough voyage. Not that I minded about that. I no longer minded about anything very much and even the fresh, salty breeze could not make me stir from the dream that gripped me. I saw the bay and the harbour and, as we drew closer, I made out at the end of the quay a steamer with three funnels which I guessed was Eli's ship. It all seemed like a picture from a book, though, or as though someone else was seeing it, and not me, William Rolandson. My limbs felt heavy with fatigue and my head ached.

The harbour was thronged with people and, as the donkey trotted towards the quayside, Eli's face clouded over and he growled with displeasure. 'Fishing trade must have picked up since I left Cornwall,' he muttered, half to himself. 'Never saw so many people waiting for the fleet to come in before.'

I think that he had meant to take the donkey cart to the very end of the quay, but we had gone only a little distance when we were surrounded by such a press of people that it was impossible for the poor little donkey to move forward, no matter how Eli beat at him with his whip.

'Devil take this confounded crowd,' he muttered, growing red in the face with anger, and then, shouting above the hubbub of women talking and children screaming, he called out : 'Mind your backs. Make way there, my beauties.' He was trying to edge the donkey cart through a group of women who must have been fishwives; they all wore shawls, and slung on their backs they carried wicker baskets. Some of them turned round and grinned cheerily at him and waved, but mostly they ignored him. One shook her fist and shouted that she wasn't moving for any donkey cart, and the others laughed. Eli swore under his breath and I saw him run his hand over his face.

'You'll not get the cart through today, sir,' said a man's voice from directly behind us. 'Where are you headed for ?'

'For the ship at the end,' Eli replied, turning round. 'If I don't hurry she'll sail without me.'

'Aye,' the man nodded, coming forward and taking hold of the donkey's bridle. I couldn't see his face, for he had a sou'wester pulled down over his eyes as though he was expecting rain. 'You'd be better on foot in this crowd,' he said. 'Have you luggage, sir?'

'Heavy boxes,' Eli growled. 'But I'll pay well for anyone who'll give me a hand with them. I never saw such a crowd here before.'

'The fleet's due back this morning,' said the fisherman. Eli nodded and pulled a sovereign out of his pocket. The next moment we were surrounded by willing helpers. Someone tried to lift me out of the cart, but Eli grabbed hold of me.

'The boy stays with me,' he said in a surly way. He jumped to the ground and lifted me down and I saw him tap his pocket and give me a meaning look. He handed me the carpet bag to carry and he pushed me ahead of him through the crowd, keeping a tight grip on my arm. Dazed though I was, my heart began to beat fast. I looked down, seeing only legs and feet as we pushed our way through the throng of people. I dared not look round, for if Samuel should be there and saw me, Eli would use the pistol, I was sure of that.

'Go on, boy, go on,' Eli whispered hoarsely in my ear. 'The ship is due to sail at any moment.' I glanced up ahead and saw Eli's trunks bobbing along, shoulder high and carried above the heads of the crowd. We must be nearly there, I thought, but the closer we came to the ship, the thicker grew the crowd until it was nearly impossible for us to move. The oddest part of all was that as we shouldered our way along, faces that I thought I knew would come and go in the crowd around me. Once I thought that I saw Hodge the pedlar, only the man was wearing a sou'wester instead of Hodge's woollen cap, so I decided I must have been mistaken. The next moment he had gone. Farther along I saw a profile that seemed to belong to the lady we had seen on the station at Plymouth, but this woman was a fishwife and wore a red shawl round her head, and carried a basket on her back. She was calling to a boy who stood on the harbour wall wearing a cloth cap and ragged trousers. I looked up, wishing I could change places with him, and thought I saw him wink at me.

Once or twice I think Eli nearly let go of me. He swore and muttered constantly in my ear, urging me to go faster, and at last I made out the gangplank just ahead of us and saw his boxes being carried aboard.

A tall seaman in uniform stepped forward to meet us.

'Mr Fennel?' he asked. 'We've been expecting you. This crowd . . . But the tide is turning, and we must go . . .'

Eli nodded. 'Only just made it in time,' he said, letting go of me at last and taking the carpet bag from my hand before he followed the seaman up the gangplank. He didn't look back until he had reached the deck. Almost at once the gangplank was raised, and the ropes which held the ship were untied. I looked up at Eli Fennel who leaned on the rail, gazing down at me, with a gleam of triumphant malice on his face. It seemed that I stayed like that for a long time as the ship slowly slipped back from the harbour wall and a widening strip of dark water separated me from him. With each moment my heart grew lighter, for I knew that I was safe from him at last. The long night was over.

'I'll send you a post card, Billy boy,' he called, raising

his bowler hat. Suddenly he began to jerk about as though he were doing a grotesque kind of jig and it was a little while before I realized that it was the tears in my eyes that made him dance like that. The tall fisherman with the red beard who stood beside me must have thought that I was sorry to see him go when he saw me crying, because he put his hand very gently on my shoulder, although he didn't say anything.

Eli Fennel waved his bowler hat at me once more. Quite quickly the ship moved out across the water, followed by the crowd of grey gulls that circled round it, and then dipping a little, it disappeared round the end of the quay.

The fisherman still had his arm round me and I looked down at his hand, wondering that a stranger should be so familiar. Then I saw how long and slender the fingers were. Surely I knew those fingers. I frowned.

'Well that's that,' said the fisherman, in quite a different voice, and he pulled off his sou'wester, very carefully indeed, and looked at me with a twinkle in his eyes. 'I don't think we'll see Eli Fennel again.'

Even now I don't know which was the more wonderful. Sometimes I think that it was discovering that the fisherman was Samuel, standing there beside me. Sometimes I think that it was looking down into the sou' wester and seeing the diamond that lay, flashing and sparkling in the bottom of the hat, returned, after all hope had gone, to its rightful owner.

13. How We Decided to Write the Story

I don't really remember very much about what happened next because everything was coming and going through a fog of tiredness. I do know that they took me back up the hill to Spindrift House and put me to bed, and from the way that Samuel kept looking at me I could tell he was worried, which seemed silly when it was all over. My mind was full of questions but I was too tired to ask any of them, and I went to sleep at once.

When I woke up the room was full of pink sunshine. Sitting beside the window and wearing her bonnet with the violets on the brim was Nellie. Her back was as straight as a ruler and her hands were folded in her lap, but on her face there was a look of rapturous wonder.

'Nellie,' I said, sitting up. 'What are you doing here?'

'A nice welcome I must say,' she said, coming over to the bed and looking at me, 'after I been sittin' there so patiently waitin' for yer to waken up. You seen all that sea?' She jerked her head towards the window. I nodded. 'All pink and gold it is,' Nellie sighed. 'I never seen anythin' so beautiful in me' life. Not much like Sandwich Bay, is it?'

'Not much,' I agreed. 'When did you get here?'

'About an hour ago. And just in time if yer ask me. One out, one in. 'Ow yer feelin' Sonny Jim?'

'All right,' I said, looking at her in surprise. Nellie only called me Sonny Jim when I was ill and I didn't know I was ill. 'A bit hungry. What d'you mean, "one out, one in"?'

Nellie sniffed. 'Never you mind,' she said. 'I told you before you're too nosey – and look where it's landed you this time!'

I grinned, but before I could reply Flora put her head round the door. 'Are you awake?' she asked. She had on a new brown dress and a huge brown ribbon on the back of her hair.

'Well 'e's awake now all right,' Nellie said.

'Quick, William, quick!' Flora said, taking hold of my hands and half dragging me out of bed. 'You must come. Gus has dismissed Mrs Turvey and she's kicking up a fearful fuss downstairs.'

'Who's Gus?' I asked.

'She's our aunt,' Flora explained, pulling me towards the door. 'Only she's called Gus because her real name's Augusta, and she's going to paint a picture of me. She said so. Look!'

We hung over the banisters on the first landing. Mrs Turvey was dressed in black as usual, with a black travelling cape and a bonnet stitched all over with black jet. Beside the front door her boxes stood ready corded.

'No,' our aunt was saying. 'It's out of the question, Mrs Turvey. After the way you treated those poor, brave children I wouldn't dream of giving you a reference. Frankly I don't consider that you're suitable to have charge of a litter of kittens.'

'Mr Rolandson said I was to tell no one where he was,' Mrs Turvey protested.

'The children,' Gus said, looking at her coldly, 'were the bearers of a message – a message, as it happened, of the utmost importance to Mr Rolandson, which they had brought here with considerable pluck and enterprise. You had no right to send them home without waiting for my return.'

Flora nudged me and grinned.

'I thought it was a prank,' Mrs Turvey said, her cheeks quivering. 'I was only doing my duty.'

'You have sadly taken advantage of me Mrs Turvey,' Gus replied, looking straight at the horrible woman. 'Was it also part of your duty to pilfer my wine? My brother tells me that the case of Beaune which he sent me last Christmas is nearly finished, and the Madeira has gone altogether. You can count yourself lucky that your "duty" has not landed you in the hands of the police.'

Mrs Turvey turned redder than ever, and the next moment she had dropped to her knees on the flagged stone floor in front of Gus. 'I beg you to overlook my little improprieties,' she babbled. 'I'll never get another position without references, Miss Rolandson, you know I won't. Have pity on me. I implore you . . .'

'Enough!' said Samuel, coming suddenly out of the drawing-room and speaking in a voice of steel as he approached the shuddering black-clad figure. 'You have stolen my sister's wine, and several of the silver teaspoons are missing. This very morning when we came back to the house we found you in the act of steaming open a telegram which was addressed to me. Heaven alone knows what else you have been guilty of. And on top of all this, you have put the lives of my dear children in deadly peril. Either you leave this house within the minute, Mrs Turvey, or I shall call Hodge in from the porch, and together we will bounce you from here to Land's End!'

Mrs Turvey raised her eyes until she could see the expression on Samuel's face, and then she knew that she had met her match. With a snarl of rage she rose to her feet, snatched up her umbrella and her portmanteau and without another word stamped off through the front door and down the drive.

'Hurrah!' Flora cried, bounding down the stairs. 'She's gone, she's gone and she'll never come back.'

'I'd like to see her try,' said Gus, laying her hands on Flora's shoulders and smiling down at her.

'I suppose you've been listening upstairs,' said Samuel, 'and I can't say I blame you.'

'For once I don't blame 'er either,' said Nellie following Flora down to the hall. 'A bad egg that Mrs Turvey if ever I saw one.' She sniffed. 'Never trust a woman with eyes like boiled gooseberries me old dad used ter say, and 'e was right.'

'Nellie,' said Samuel with a twinkle in his eye, 'it's quite clear that you intend to stay, so why don't you take your bonnet off? Where's William?'

'I'm here,' I said from the landing. They all turned and stared up at me then, which made me feel rather foolish as I had nothing on but my nightshirt.

'Is he all right?' Samuel asked, turning to Nellie.

'Did all that noise wake him up?' Gus asked.

'Perhaps he should go back to bed,' Samuel suggested.

'No, thank you,' I said firmly, leaning on the banisters. 'I'm wide awake and perfectly well, and I wish you'd all stop behaving as though I wasn't here and tell me when there'll be some tea or supper, or something because I feel very hungry.'

'Unmistakable signs of complete recovery,' said Samuel solemnly. 'Why don't you go and get dressed William, so that you can come down and meet your aunt properly?'

'Hello, William,' said Gus, smiling up at me.

'Hello,' I said. 'I've seen you before. On Plymouth Station. And I think I saw you this morning as well, but I'm not sure ...'

'Ah,' said Gus with a little nod. 'What a great deal we all have to say to each other – but not until after supper.'

'Yes,' said Nellie, pulling hat pins out of her bonnet, 'and that's my department I shouldn't wonder, so quick's the word and sharp's the action.'

We had supper in the kitchen and afterwards Gus led us into her drawing-room where we sat in a circle round the log fire which burned in the huge grate. It was hard to decide who should begin because we all had so much to tell and so many questions to ask, but in the end it was agreed that, since everything had started with Samuel, he should begin at the beginning. So he told the others the story that Eli Fennel had told me about the finding of the diamond and the journey to the coast, and of how Eli had stolen the stone. When he had finished, we all sat quiet for a minute, and then Flora stirred.

'But why did he do it?' she asked, her eyes wide as she looked at Samuel.

'Greed,' said Samuel sadly. 'There was more than enough for both of us and I would willingly have shared it with him, for he was my angel. Instead he stole it all.'

'Angel?' Flora asked.

'More like Devil I'd say,' Nellie sniffed.

'Well, it comes to the same thing,' Samuel smiled. 'That's why I called him Lucifer you see – after the angel who fell from heaven. And I daresay that Eli has been in hell, more or less, ever since. When I saw him on the quayside this morning I barely recognized him. I never saw a man so changed.' Samuel looked into the fire for a long time until Flora tapped him on the knee.

'What happened after Eli stole the diamond?' she prompted.

'Well, I made my way to the coast, as you know,' Samuel went on. 'I must have cut a pretty tragic figure, I daresay, for I had lost the two things in the world that were most precious to me. My best friend – for he *was* my best friend, believe it or not – and a fortune. But then, look what I'd found,' he smiled, laying a hand on my shoulder, for I was sitting on the ground beside him.

'During the journey to the coast I had time to think and I worked out a plan, for I didn't mean to let Eli get off scot free I may tell you. As soon as I arrived I put the story about, for I knew that before long it would be sure to reach him and he would realize that I had not been devoured by vultures as he had hoped, but was quite safe and sound and on his trail. Then, after some little delay I took ship for England. There were storms around the Cape of Good Hope which delayed me, and Eli arrived home before I did. I knew, you see, what he would do, for he really had no alternative. I was certain that he would go home to Cornwall, and there he would hide the stone so that one day he could return for it. If he had tried to sell it then he would have been recognized, and knowing the diamond's history, no one would have bought it. When I arrived in Cornwall I made enquiries in the neighbourhood and I learnt that he had, indeed, been home, but that he had gone away again, this time to Australia, some said. Then I knew that my guess had been right and that it was merely a question of biding my time, for one day he would come home again and collect the diamond. I never dreamed, though, that it would be such a long wait.'

'I think that this is where I come into the story isn't it?' Gus asked him, with a mischievous little smile.

'I thought it was your turn to prompt me,' Samuel

replied, smiling. 'There were ten of us at home,' he went on, 'and the other eight brothers and sisters were pretty well behaved. Gus and I were always – '

'Lively?' Gus suggested.

Samuel nodded. 'Our parents didn't like young people to be independent,' he went on. 'They would have preferred us to continue driving around the smoky north and paying calls on boring people. I made my escape first. I enlisted in the army and went to India. I served for upwards of eight years, and then, tiring of the life, I sold my commission and went to Africa where, it was said, there were diamonds for the taking.' He smiled. 'Gus had to wait a few years after I left home. Then a fairy godmother came along and swept her off to Paris to study art. Later, when the time came for her to settle down somewhere, she asked me where to go. I suggested Cornwall. There were several artists living in this part of the world already, which suited her, since critics, like starlings, go in flocks. So while she painted, she watched and listened. I, unfortunately, having no fairy godmother, and no money either when I returned from Africa, had to make my way as best I could – which was how I drifted into the Music Hall and became an illusionist. But that you all know.'

'And have you been waiting for Eli to come home all this time?' Flora asked.

Samuel laughed. 'When at last Gus heard that he was expected, she dispatched Joel Tregarth to me with a letter. Joel was one of the few people we trusted, and he knew a little of the matter, but no one knew very much, for it wasn't safe to say a great deal. The stone had been stolen once and could easily be stolen again.'

'And that was what the letter was about?' Flora asked. 'The one that Joel brought?'

'Yes. Seeing that there was no time to be lost, I packed my bag, wrote a note to all of you and left immediately.'

'But what about the packet?' I asked.

'That was when things began to go wrong,' Samuel nodded. 'No sooner had Joel arrived back at the Port of London than he saw Eli. Realizing that Eli must have slipped ashore several days earlier than had been anticipated, and that it would change my plans a good deal, he wrote me a letter and enclosed with it a list of the steamship sailings from Penzance and Newlyn during the course of the next three or four days. Then he walked back at first light and delivered the package. Gus and I had thought originally that Eli would try to sail from Plymouth . . .'

'And that's why we saw you on the platform there,' I interrupted, looking at Gus.

'Yes,' she said. 'I had to go there to find out the steamship sailings. It was the only way we could get them. And that's why I wasn't here when you arrived, because I had to spend the night in Plymouth and travel back the following morning.'

'If you'd been here,' Flora said, 'everything would have been all right.'

'That's jumping ahead a bit though,' Samuel said. 'Where had we got to?'

'To that man arrivin' wiv the package,' Nellie said with a sniff.

'Oh, yes,' Samuel smiled. 'Poor Joel was in a bit of bother then, and when you two offered to bring the packet down to me yourselves it must have seemed like a gift from heaven. He wasn't to know what a chapter of accidents would follow.'

'It was all my fault,' Flora said gloomily, 'for choosing Eli's carriage.'

'I think it was a miracle that you managed to catch the train at all,' Samuel said. 'I am deeply grateful to you both for undertaking such an errand – and I am very proud of you.'

'I never thought you'd be proud of me,' Flora murmured, her eyes shining.

'Well, I am tonight,' said Samuel seriously. 'I think you have both been exceedingly brave. It must have been very frightening to arrive here and find neither me, nor Gus.'

'Only that horrid Mrs Turvey,' said Flora quietly.

'Well, if it weren't for you two, and the courage and wit that you both showed, I should not have the diamond in my safe keeping tonight,' Samuel said looking from one to the other of us. 'You see, as soon as I discovered from the papers that were in the packet that there was a boat sailing for Rotterdam in the morning I was certain that Eli intended to be on it, and with the diamond. Rotterdam is the main trading centre for diamonds from all over the world. By then I had guessed that he would hold William as a hostage.' He laid his hand gently on my shoulder. 'Looking for you on the moors at night would have been like looking for a needle in a haystack. But on the harbour, in broad daylight I couldn't miss you. Waiting until morning seemed the only thing to do. Where did he take you William?'

'To Ding Dong,' I said quietly, looking at the sparks flying up the chimney. The memory was still too fresh for me to be able to tell the story without a shudder of fear, but I managed to get everything in, I think. Nellie sat with her mouth open, and Flora clutched my hand tight when I told them how Eli had lowered me on the end of the rope into the depths of the shaft.

Samuel and Gus looked at one another, and when I

had finished, Gus shivered. 'It passes belief,' she said in a low voice. 'If . . .'

'Sh . . . sh . . .' Samuel said, shaking his head. 'It's over. Let it lie.'

'Yes,' she agreed. 'We mustn't think of it.'

'I'd like to know why Gus was on the harbour dressed up as a fishwife,' I said, lightly, trying to forget the darkness of the moor and the cold chill of the shaft.

'Ah, yes,' said Samuel, glancing at me. 'Well as to that, you must understand that I realized the only way to recover the diamond was to wait until Eli reached the harbour. Unfortunately I realized, too, that he would certainly be expecting me to be there. That was why I was dressed as a fisherman and was wearing that red beard that you and Flora thought so absurd. Eli had only known me cleanshaven, so it seemed a fair enough disguise. The problem was how to recover the diamond without his knowing what we were doing. There was only one way, and so, hey presto . . .' Samuel waved his hand, 'I magicked a great crowd of people on to the quay.'

'I don't understand,' I interrupted.

'Well, let me go on and you will,' Samuel said. 'My crowd were a few of Hodge's friends who agreed, for a small consideration, to play the game. When we discovered that the fishing fleet was due in as well it was a real stroke of good fortune. We dressed Gus up as a fishwife, and Flora became a little ragged boy, to her great delight.'

'I winked at you,' Flora said. 'I was up on the wall.'

'I thought I'd dreamed it,' I said.

'Hodge was there too,' Samuel went on, 'and I was close beside you all the time, although you never knew it. Closer to you than I am now.'

'But I still don't understand how you managed to

get the diamond,' I said.

Samuel pulled a face. 'Really,' he protested, 'can't an Illusionist have any secrets? Suffice it to say that by the time Eli Fennel reached the gangplank, the stone was in my sou'wester and he was none the wiser.'

'Samuel!' I said, looking up at him. 'You picked his pocket.'

'Not exactly his pocket,' Samuel smiled. 'He carried the stone in a more awkward place than that – next to his heart actually. Recovering it from that stony place was no easy matter I can tell you.'

'Isn't it wonderful?' Flora cried excitedly, clapping her hands together. 'The Astonishing Rolandson. No one could have done it but you.'

'Very likely not,' said Samuel with natural pride. 'It's all a matter of practice – and flair of course.' We all laughed, and Samuel looked rather surprised, until Flora nearly smothered him by flinging her arms round him and kissing him very often.

'What will Eli do?' I asked, a bit later, 'when he finds out?'

'There is nothing he can do,' Samuel replied. 'He won't come back. And if he does he won't find it, for I don't intend to keep the diamond myself. That would be ridiculous.' We were about to protest I think, Flora and I, but Samuel suddenly looked very serious. 'You see,' he went on, 'it's amongst the six most valuable stones in the world. Only an Indian Rajah would be rich enough to buy it – or possibly the Tzar of all the Russias. I shall take it up to London in the morning and put it in the hands of a diamond dealer. I shan't handle the matter myself at all . . .'

'Well, aren't we goin' ter get a look at this fantastical stone?' Nell asked suddenly. 'I 'aven't seen it at all yet, and I won't b'lieve in it till I do.'

Samuel laughed and nodded to Gus, who stood up and went over to the Chinese cabinet. Presently she came back with the diamond, which was lying on a little silk cushion. She put it on a low stool in front of the fire and we sat in a circle and gazed at it. For a long time there was silence. In size and shape and colour it was breathtaking and none of us could think of anything to say.

'Come,' said Gus a little uneasily at last. 'Let's put it away now. It's not good to look at such richness for too long. Beside it everything else seems shabby.' She wrapped it up carefully once more in the piece of silk she held in her hand, and took it back to the cabinet. 'I'm going to make some hot chocolate,' she said, when she had locked it away. 'Flora, will you help me?'

They went out together leaving the three of us sitting beside the fire. After a while Nellie nodded off to sleep. She always did at this time of night.

'Let's go and look at the stars,' Samuel whispered, and together we crept across the room and opened the long windows into the garden. 'They seem so much brighter here than they do in London,' Samuel said, as we looked up at the sky which was twinkling above us. 'I suppose that's an illusion too.'

'Was he really your best friend?' I asked suddenly.

'Yes,' Samuel nodded. 'That was the hardest thing to bear. Poor Eli, he could have done so much, and it's all been wasted.'

'Yes,' I said. 'I think I feel sorry for him too.' I paused. 'There's another thing I want to ask you,' I said. 'Eli told me that I reminded him of someone. Do you know who it was?'

'It was your mother, I think,' Samuel answered after a pause. 'I've never told you about it before, but you're old enough now to know the truth. She was Dutch.

Her husband had been killed by a band of Zulus, and she was travelling back to the coast with our party to return to her parents in Holland. You were with her. I suppose you were two months old.'

'Was she pretty?' I asked.

'Yes,' said Samuel. 'She was dark. She had your eyes and your funny, tipped up nose, but she didn't smile as often as you do. Eli grew very fond of her I think. But . . .' Samuel sighed. 'When the moment came he loved the diamond more than any human being.'

'I'm glad you told me,' I said. 'Thank you Samuel.'

'That's the polar star,' he said after a moment, putting his hand on my shoulder and pointing up at the blue-black sky. 'The one you steer by when you're at sea.' He smiled at me. 'That ship must be halfway to Rotterdam by now, and do you realize that if it wasn't for you and Flora, Eli would be down in his cabin gloating over the diamond at this very moment. Now that wouldn't be at all the right ending, would it?'

'It would make a good story,' I said thoughtfully.

'You'd better write it then,' Samuel said.

When we told Flora she looked quite shocked.

'We couldn't possibly do that,' she said. 'It would take far too long. Besides, what would we call it?'

'That's easy,' said Samuel. 'You could call it *The Lucifer Stone*.'

So we did.

It took even longer than Flora had thought it would to write, but as we're having the whole summer off school and staying with Gus we've had plenty of time.

Now that Samuel's sold the diamond and we've got so much money, he suggested that we might go round the world by boat in the autumn, but then, travelling doesn't always seem such a very good thing. Flora's quite upset to think of all the dancing classes she would miss, and Nellie says she'd be certain to be seasick. Gus said she'd miss us all far too much anyway, and she couldn't possibly allow us to go, so I don't suppose we will.

I don't know what we'll do instead, but I think it would be fine just to go on being beside the sea, because then I could go out fishing with Joel Tregarth every day – and the silly thing is that you don't need to be rich at all to do that. Actually I'm going fishing with Joel right now, so I think this is a good place to end the story.

The Warden's Niece

GILLIAN AVERY

Maria hated school. She couldn't do her lessons and the threat of having to wear a label marked 'slut' for blotchy work was the last straw. So, on the 18th May 1875, she decided to run away. And as her secret ambition was to be a professor at Oxford, it was not unnatural for her to escape to her uncle, the Warden of Canterbury College.

That was the beginning of a wildly adventurous summer with the three Smith brothers, aided and abetted by their splendidly eccentric tutor. But it was a summer when the Warden's niece proved to herself, the dusty scholars and the boys – who would grudgingly admit that she was slightly better than most girls – that she too could carry out a proper piece of research, gather together the clues and solve a mystery quite by herself.

A Likely Lad and *The Greatest Gresham* are also Lions.

Gillian Avery's books are for ten-year-olds and upwards.

No Way of Telling

EMMA SMITH

Amy and her grandmother were tucked in safely, happy in the warmth of their mountain cottage while the blizzard raged outside. Then Mick growled . . . The door burst open, and there stood a shape so big that to Amy it was more of a monster than a man. He said nothing, only grabbed some food and disappeared again into the stormy darkness.

Who was he? Would he come back? And was he the hunter or the hunted? Amy and her grandmother had no way of telling. A gripping story for older readers.

Emma Smith was shortlisted for the 1973 Carnegie Medal for this story of suspense and fear set in the Welsh mountains.